WITHDRAW

BY ELIZABETH BORTON DE TREVIÑO

THE HEART POSSESSED

THE HEART POSSESSED

A LOVE STORY

Elizabeth Borton de Treviño

DOUBLEDAY & COMPANY, INC.
GARDEN CITY, NEW YORK
1978

English translation by Lorna de' Lucchi of part of *La Vita Nuova* by Dante, from *An Anthology of Italian Poets*. Reprinted by permission of Alfred A. Knopf, Inc., and William Heinemann, Ltd.

Library of Congress Cataloging in Publication Data

Treviño, Elizabeth Borton, 1904–
  The heart possessed.

  I. Title.
PZ3.T72844He [PS3539.R455] 813'.5'2
ISBN: 0-385-03536-5
Library of Congress Catalog Card Number 77–26523

To Sally Arteseros

Tanto gentile e tanto onesta pare
la donna mia, quand' ella altrui saluta,
ch' ogni lingua deven tremando muta,
e li occhi no l' ardiscon di guardare.
Ella si va, sentendosi laudare,
benignamente d' umiltà vestuta;
e par che sia una cosa venuta
da cielo in terra a miracol mostrare.
Mostrasi si piacente a chi la mira
che da per li occhi una dolcezza al core,
che 'nentender no la può chi no la prova;
e par che de la sua labbia si mova
un spirito soave e pien d'amore,
che va dicendo a l'anima: "Sospira."

DANTE ALIGHIERI, *La Vita Nuova.*

Translation by Lorna de' Lucchi

So gentle and so pure appears to me
My Lady, when she greeting doth bestow,
That every tongue is hushed in ecstasy
And eyes for awe their heritage forgo.
She passeth, hearing how she is admired,
Benignly, all regardless of her worth;
It is as if she were a thing inspired,
A miracle by heaven shown on earth.
She is so beautiful to see that by
A glance the heart is soothed in such sweet way
As only he who knows can truly say:
And from her lips a spirit seems to move,
A spirit filled with tenderness and love,
Forever saying to the soul, "Ah, sigh."

THE HEART POSSESSED

Prologue

The shadows had lengthened across the close-cut emerald grass, and a light breeze from the sea was beginning to move the tops of the pines and cypresses. White-coated attendants were taking in the lawn chairs, and nurses were coaxing a few reluctant patients in toward closed terraces of the hospital.

The building itself looked homelike and attractive. It was built like an antebellum mansion, with tall columns sustaining an upper balcony (the doctors' lounge), and the reception rooms and visitors' rooms, on the first floor, were spacious, furnished with carved fruitwood sofas, chairs, and tables, and always fragrant with flowers. The wards, treatment rooms, doctors' offices, and private rooms extended far to the rear, in a sort of steel-bound box, for security, but were not visible from the front, or from the lawns.

Inside the hospital proper, doctors were gathering up their notes, glancing at their watches, and preparing to meet in the lounge, to discuss their cases. It was Friday afternoon.

Young Dr. Francis Sullivan was one of the first to arrive. The latest doctor to be placed on staff, he took meticulous care of all the required details of his residency, because of his intense interest in the work he was doing. He was still full of hope.

As the doctors gathered, Mrs. Williams, the housekeeper, brought a tray of cups and a pot of coffee. Dr. Greenberg, chief of staff, took his place at the head of the oval table where the other doctors had already found their seats. Dr. Greenberg was in his fifties, but still had a head of thick and curling hair. His lined face was swarthy, and at this time of day had already begun to show that he needed a shave. He rustled his papers impatiently. Dr. Greenberg's wife was giving a dinner party at their home, twenty miles away, and he was determined not to fail her this time, as he had the last time. Social amenities meant a great deal to her, and she was younger than he by fifteen years.

Dr. Abraham Hirsch, blond and full of jokes, looked younger than his forty years, perhaps because of his unshakable good humor. He was in charge of the violent patients. Seabright Hospital, being a private institution, could choose or reject patients. It did not accept patients with a history of violence or aggression, but sometimes the mildest case turned difficult. For these, nobody was better than Dr. Hirsch, who, besides being naturally agreeable, was also fearless.

Dr. Roderick Phillips, handsome in a dark, clean-featured way, tall and graceful in his bearing, was in charge of the Women's Ward. Dr. Marian Chester, somewhat plump and matronly in appearance, softly pretty, with thick brown hair growing down to her collar, and with large gentle brown eyes, was his assistant.

Dr. John Tomlinson, who had come to Seabright from the State Hospital, had the Men's Ward, and was also in charge of general plans of medication. Francis Sullivan, short, blond, and freckled, with blue eyes behind his glasses, was his assistant.

Dr. Greenberg looked around quickly.

"Anything important . . . new to report?" he asked. At once everyone knew he wanted to get away quickly.

Dr. Phillips nodded a negative.

"Marian?"

"I have to repeat my request, Dr. Greenberg. Every month at full moon I can't get them to sleep. Couldn't I have a ration of hot milk to give each one, with sugar? They would love it, and it would help so much . . ." Her eager voice tapered away into silence.

"Management tells me we are running close to the line, and management wants profits," he answered. "Why don't you try to fix it with Williams to hold out the milk from the lunch menu and let you have it at night? Finagle it some way."

Dr. Phillips hid his faint smile behind his hand. Dr. Chester had been doing that, all the last week, with his connivance. He could get around Williams. Middle-aged women were easy for him.

"Dr. Sullivan?"

Francis started.

"I have a new patient, that is, *we* have," he began. "A woman, she should be under Dr. Phillips's care, but I have asked to have her under my supervision."

Dr. Phillips spoke. "Francis is paying the fees for the woman, so I let him have her."

Dr. Greenberg frowned.

"This is . . ."

"I don't think it is irregular," put in Dr. Sullivan hastily, a bit breathlessly. "She is no relation. I just found her. And the case is remarkably interesting, so I wanted to treat her. She seems to be completely alone, no family, nobody. I am gladly covering her fees."

Dr. Greenberg smiled. He had had the same enthusiasm and idealism years ago.

"Is she beautiful?" he asked.

3

"Very," put in Dr. Phillips.

"And I suppose she thinks she is Helen of Troy," murmured Dr. Greenberg, gathering his papers together. "Or Cleopatra."

"No, not exactly," said Dr. Sullivan. "She thinks she is a saint."

PART I

San Francisco, 1926

1
DR. SULLIVAN

Francis Brady Sullivan was a San Franciscan. He loved
every inch of his city, from the dirty streets "South of the
Slot" to the elegance of Russian Hill. He loved the clan-
gor of Market Street, the screech of the cable car around
corners, the exotic smells of Chinatown, the thick fogs
that rolled in from the sea, the bay, the bridges, and the
Marina.

His father had been a successful lawyer, who had
hoped to leave his practice and his law library to his
oldest son. But it turned out that Martin, the younger son,
had inherited his drive, his interest in the intricacies of
the law. Francis had announced, the very year he finished
high school, that he wanted to be a doctor, a psychiatrist.

"Good God, you can see all the crazy people you want,
practicing law," his father had protested. But Francis's
mother understood something about why her oldest son
was attracted to the study of people who were unsure of
reality, or appalled by it, and why work in a hospital
seemed natural to him. A slight limp was all that remained of Francis's five years in various hospitals as a
young boy, due to a stubborn infection in the bone of his
leg. His mother, a devoted and dutiful Catholic, had
prayed for him constantly, and he had known it. Her own
confidence and piety had bolstered the boy's wavering
faith, and the end, when an operation was undertaken, in
full cognizance of the medical warnings—that he might
die, that in any case he might never walk again—the little
boy's calm certainty that he would get better undoubt-
edly helped in some strange way. To the doctors, his re-

covery seemed mysterious; to his mother, it was miraculous but definitely to be attributed to the angels, into whose care she had given him.

Francis had done well at medical school, and had never entertained a moment's doubt that this was the course for his life. Companions who had started out with him fell by the wayside, because they found that the life of a doctor was extremely difficult and demanding. Others stayed with it, in the hope of earning plenty of money. It was not lost on many of the medical students, that doctors earned more than individuals in any other profession. Those who persisted through and into the psychiatric specialty were, Francis had explained to his mother, in one of three categories. They were stubborn, and intended to stick to the phase of medicine likely to yield a fortune sooner than any other, and without the risks of surgery; or they were carried into the specialty by the presence of some member of their family who was mentally afflicted or unbalanced; or they really had a vocation for the work.

"And you, Frankie, have the vocation," she finished. Mary Brady Sullivan, a widow now, was a little blond woman, and he resembled her, but whereas he was not a handsome man, she had been very pretty in her youth, with flyaway golden hair, dark blue eyes, and deep dimples in rose-leaf cheeks.

"Perhaps a bit of the family interest, too," he reminded her. "You recall the story of Uncle Tim?"

"Oh yes." Mrs. Sullivan was suddenly serious. Then her eyes filled slowly with tears.

"I always loved him," she said.

Uncle Tim, in Mrs. Sullivan's girlhood in a little town in Maine, had gone to sea, returning infrequently, shouldering his sea chest. But one year when he came home, he was vague and morose; other sailors on the voyage reported that he had had a bad fall on the deck during a storm.

Uncle Tim had never spoken again, but lived, off and on, in the Brady home, carrying his plate of food out to the little harness room in back, where he lived, with the family horse, used for plowing. Little Mary had often gone out to the harness room, put her small hand in his, and taken Uncle Tim for walks. She chattered happily with him, but he never answered, though he often sighed. In the spring he helped with plowing and planting; in the winter he carved little figurines from wood or shell.

He had perished in a snowstorm, into which he had charged, desperately, when he had been told that Mary was lost. The child was brought home by a neighbor, but Uncle Tim was not found for thirty hours, and by then he was frozen stiff. Mary had never forgotten the sad figure of Uncle Tim, nor the way he had been teased, on occasion, by the village children.

After their mother had told them the story of Uncle Tim, Martin had laughed. "Crazy old coot," he had remarked. Martin was only seven, and Francis nine. But the story stayed with Francis. In California, the boy had never seen a snowstorm, but the San Francisco fogs used to recall the story to him, and he could imagine the desperate figure of the silent man, searching for the lost child, through the veils of mist.

"Probably with X-rays and good care, he could have been helped," Francis said now.

"They discover new things all the time," murmured his mother.

They two looked at each other with understanding, and she patted his arm affectionately.

9

Francis had been overjoyed at his appointment to Seabright, though he planned to go into private practice after some six to ten years gaining a broad experience in the hospital.

"There's so much to learn, Ma," he told her. "There are so many mysteries, still. People who get better, we don't know why, and other people who by every rule we know ought to be recovering, sink deeper and deeper into a sort of half-life, sometimes almost no conscious life at all."

"You'll learn it," his mother proclaimed confidently. "And besides, I pray for you every day."

Francis had not the direct childish piety of his mother, but he believed that doctors have to have divine aid in their work. In his own difficult specialty, he felt certain that heavenly guidance—call it intuition, chance, or fate—could mean the difference between treating a case with confidence and feeling his way through a maze of tangled doubts.

Mrs. Sullivan was eager for her Frankie to marry, and regularly produced eligible young ladies, Catholics, good girls who had been brought up to feel strong family loyalties.

"I don't care if they can cook or keep house," she told him once. "I can teach any girl how to run a house and a kitchen. I want a girl that will march shoulder to shoulder with you, not one of those flibbertigibbets that want to run out the minute there's any trouble. Loyalty, that's what counts in a marriage. Loyalty and love."

"Ma. Those wonderful girls aren't going to want a guy like me," he teased. He had no plans to marry, and had never been deeply in love. He had had girls, had experimented, as young men do. Martin, younger, but naturally more amorous, had asked him once if so much medical knowledge about women had made him impotent.

"Oh, I don't think so," Francis had answered mildly.

"Well, you are missing a lot," commented Martin, who pursued girls with constant interest and had had several intense affairs.

Francis had gone his way, untroubled, never dreaming that he would one day have to struggle with an emotion that could overpower him.

Until a wet dark day in June, when he was visiting an outpatient clinic in South San Francisco.

He sat in as observer while a colleague took care of the patients who came in for talks and medicine. Most of them seemed normal enough, until the doctor asked a question that probed the obsession, or touched briefly on a hallucination. The last patient was a girl of about thirteen, who came in shivering and crying. A young woman dressed in dark clothes accompanied her, and tried gently to comfort her, patting her, lifting the small hand and kissing it.

"Now Florence, no need to be afraid," said Dr. Cummins. "I am not going to give you an injection today. We will just have a little chat."

The girl quieted almost at once, and the talk was routine. Francis could not take his eyes off the young woman who accompanied the patient. She looked up once, full at him, and he got a sudden impression of perfect loveliness. Her face was oval, pale, unlined, set in a mold of dignity and sadness. Her hair was dark brown, combed back from a broad forehead. Under level dark brows, her eyes were a large shining gray, fringed with dark lashes. She wore no make-up and the shape of her lips was curved and tender.

A Correggio madonna, thought Francis.

She didn't say a word, and after she and the patient had left and Dr. Cummins was ready to close the clinic, Francis asked about the young woman.

"She's a mystery," said the doctor. "That is, nobody knows anything about her. She's crazy, but not certifiable. We can't do anything for her because she won't talk. She seems to have no home. She goes around taking care of anybody who is sick or in trouble . . . scrubs floors, cooks, waits on them. Sleeps on the floor, wherever she is. You're a San Franciscan, you know about the Emperor? Perfectly mad old codger who went about doing acts of charity. The whole city knew him, knew that he was scrupulously honest and that he knew where to help. So even city money was entrusted to him, to administrate for the poor. Well, this woman seems to be the same type. Everybody knows her, and she is trusted."

"What's her name?"

"Who knows? Some people call her Margaret."

"Is she a nun?"

"No. We've checked around. No, she just lives this way because she wants to. Eats scraps, whatever is around. She goes and takes care of some of the most dreadful old people, dirty, you know, and smelly, she seems to seek this sort of thing. Well, we need her, and more like her, until the government gets around to doing something for the aged poor."

"Doesn't anyone know where she came from?" persisted Francis. He felt drawn to the strange girl.

"No, she's a mystery."

After consulting with his friend Dr. Cummins, Francis arranged to be often at the clinic, and he was thus able to learn more about where Margaret went, and where she might be. When he could, he quietly helped her about her nursing tasks. She never spoke, but he began to feel that he was gaining her confidence.

It seemed to him that all his professional training had prepared him to fathom the enigma of Margaret's behavior, and he was determined to cure her.

Mrs. Sullivan loved her two sons with an equal devotion but she had a deeper intuitive understanding of her son Francis. Given a basic fact, or thought, she knew how his mind worked because her own followed the same patterns. Her grandmother in Ireland had had "the sight," a Celtic sensitivity to the thoughts of other people, and Mary Sullivan had inherited the gift, which made itself felt on odd and unrelated occasions. Most often, she experienced, in her own mind, Francis's thoughts.

He depended on this quality of identification in his mother, and on her deep and ever-ready sympathy, and he often talked over his cases with her.

When he first mentioned the girl Margaret to his mother, Mary Sullivan felt as if a hand had closed gently around her heart.

"She is pitiful, but she has dignity, Ma," her son told her. "She reminds me of some medieval painting; there is a curiously classic look to her face. Like a sixteenth-century madonna."

Mary felt a surge of defensive love for her son. Dear Frankie. So serious, so dedicated, so vulnerable despite his learning, and the insights of his profession.

He loves her, Mary thought. He has fallen in love. I know it. And therefore, this girl has power to hurt him, because he has never loved before.

"I want to cure her," he told his mother. "I am sure

13

there is a fine, a splendid person in her, there inside, that could be released into life, freed from a web of dreams. I want to cure her! I believe I can!"

"Oh, you will," his mother told him. "I know you will!"

Then came his appointment to Seabright, and he was not able to get away, to visit his family, to try to trace the mysterious Margaret as often as he wished. Whenever he could, he took time to look for her. She had become an obsession with him; he saw her beautiful, sad face in his dreams, and longed to know more about her. She seemed to be an apparition from another century; there was a legendary quality to her strange beauty.

On a rainy wintry afternoon, he received a telephone call from San Francisco while in his office at Seabright.

"Frankie? Cummins. Well, your mysterious lady . . . she is sick and unconscious here. Why don't you come and get her?"

Francis did not hesitate a moment.

"Where? Where is she?"

"I've got her here in the clinic."

"I'll be there in an hour."

And so he had brought her to Seabright.

She was very ill, with pneumonia and the effects of starvation for some weeks, but as she began to recover, Francis learned that she sometimes talked to herself, and often prayed aloud. He began arriving at her bed regularly when she said her prayers, and joining her in them, blessing his mother for having had him thoroughly taught by the nuns. His reward came after almost ten days of this, when she turned to him with a smile as she whispered, "Amen."

14

It was a beautiful smile, he thought, worth the weeks of waiting. It was a true smile, a giving of the spirit.

Leaning forward, "Margaret," he said, "tell me your name, all your name."

"I am Margaret of Cortona," she whispered, after a time. Then she turned away from him and would say no more.

Francis phoned his mother, late that night.

"Ma. Wasn't there a saint named Margaret?"

"Oh yes. Several. Margaret of Scotland, St. Margaret Mary, Margaret of Cortona . . ."

"That's the one, Ma. Margaret of Cortona. Tell me about her."

"Well . . . let me think. She was a medieval saint. In Italy. She led a sinful life, as I recall, and her brothers ambushed and killed her lover. St. Margaret's dog led her to where they had hastily buried him. Then she gave herself up to work among the sick poor, and she is known as a great penitent . . . That's all I can remember. But I can get you more details. Father Bernini at Christ the King Church has a great big book about all the saints. Do you want me to?"

"Yes, Ma. When you have time. Please. But you've given me enough to go on for now."

"She is always shown with her dog, I remember that part."

"What kind of a dog?"

"A big dog. Some kind of big hunting dog."

"Thanks, Ma."

2

JOHN WADE

Well, Doctor, I run a little mission in a poor section of San Francisco, as you see. We get many Negroes, some Italian, some Irish, many plain Americans down on their luck, or trying to get off drugs by themselves, or too old and ignorant to know where to go to get some help. You would think the government would work something out to help these derelicts, washed up on a lonely shore, you might say, but it doesn't. Not yet. And I sometimes wonder if it would be the best thing. I know many people think the government has an obligation to see that no citizen is in dire need, but when that day comes—and mind you, I think it will come—what happens to Christian charity? Ordinary citizens will then say, I pay my taxes, let the government take care of them. And the necessary help will be given without love.

We have no regular funds. No church group backs us. It is just something I do, with whoever feels like giving me a hand. I have a place. Well, it was a livery stable, but horses have been out of style for about fifteen years, I guess. I fixed up the front section as a kind of living room, a place where tired people can stop and rest their feet. We have a gas stove, where we make soup, coffee, or chocolate. And in the back, I have a few cots and even some straw mattresses. You'd be surprised how many desperate people need a place to sleep, especially on a rainy or cold night.

Drunks? Yes, of course. Lots of them. Unless they are mean, I treat them just like the rest. The cop on the beat here knows me and what I do, and he looks in every now and then to make sure I don't have any real trouble.

Yes, I have a little money. This livery stable belonged to my father. He left it to me, and there was something in the bank too. There's no reason why you should know why I got into this work. It's a long story, and sad in the telling, so let's pass over that. You want me to tell you about this woman. The one who began to stop in here every now and then, just quietly doing whatever was needed at the moment.

I remember the first time I saw her. That was about four months ago. It was July, and had been cold all day. You know, July is a cold month here; the Alaska current turns and comes in close to our shores, and we get a taste of icy winter in summer. The door was steamy, and I was making cocoa. The Ghirardelli people often send me over a case of their sweetened cocoa, and I make it with as much milk as I can get my hands on. Anyhow, it is hot and sweet, and keeps out the chill.

I felt the cold draft from the door, and turned to see who had seen our sign. It says, "Welcome. Free coffee." Only of course, it isn't always coffee.

She stood in the door, looking at me with a strange expression, and she was breathing hard as if she had been running.

"Come in," I said. "Welcome."

She hurriedly shut the door, and looked around as if she were seeing things for the first time. I mean, she acted like somebody from another planet. Or out of another age. I don't know how to explain it. Startled and curious and wondering.

She herself didn't look as if she needed what we have to give. She was wearing a long dark dress, very plain,

17

with a tight scarf of dark silk tied around her head, hiding the hair.

But I saw the clothes in a glimpse, and they were of no interest. What held me, startled me, were her eyes. Very large eyes, the color of a sea fog at dusk . . . such a light gray that they would have seemed almost blind except for the thin black line outlining the iris, and the thick dark lashes that shadowed them.

"Can I get you some chocolate?"

She shook her head but she went at once to the stove, and simply took over. She poured out into our cups what we had, and passed the chocolate around. When it was gone, she went out in back to where we have a little sink and faucet, and washed and dried them, and came to put them back. I saw her busily getting some coffee ready in the big enamel pot.

"You've been a help," I said, when nobody seemed to need anything for a few minutes.

"May I stay here tonight?" she asked suddenly. She had seen the cots inside. "I can look after people, anyone who comes in, clean up in the morning . . ."

Her voice was gentle, of medium pitch, and educated. I couldn't detect any accent, so I supposed she must be a Californian, like myself.

"Of course. This mission is just for anybody who has to have a hot drink and a place to sleep. Anybody."

She lay down, with her clothes on of course, and seemed to sleep. Anyhow, she lay there quietly. I looked in a few times. In the morning she was up early making coffee, and she stepped around my improvised kitchen and wielded broom and mop and washed dishes, like any housewife.

We never ask anybody for his name, so I didn't ask her.

But I thought she might tell me. Or reveal something about herself. She didn't. And at about ten, she quietly left. I didn't see her again for days. However, some of the regulars who came to the mission told me about her. She appeared wherever she seemed to be needed, especially to the old and sick people who had no one to look after them. She bathed them and cleaned their rooms, often lay down to sleep there herself, usually on the floor, they said.

Her name, they told me, was Margaret. In the neighborhood, they thought that she was a nursing nun who had left her convent for some reason. But she never spoke about herself.

She didn't come back, and I missed her. I found myself thinking about her a lot, and I could close my eyes and see her. Beautiful? Well, no, I wouldn't say so, except for the lovely eyes. It seemed to me to be just an ordinary face, rather pale. Of course, I never saw her hair.

What's your interest in her, Doctor? Was she a nurse, or what?

I see. You want to find out more about her, trace her, learn something about her life. Well, I can't help you there. But if she should appear around here again, I'll let you know. Where can I get in touch with you?

Thanks. I'll put your card right here on the wall by the calendar. That way I won't lose it.

Clues. Yes, I see what you mean. Well, I would say, yes, she is a Californian. Another thing, she must know San Francisco well. Either she was born here, or she lived here sometime. And she had certainly had money, because her clothes were not shoddy or badly cut. But, aside from those observations . . .

Yes. Any time. Let me know if you find out something more about Margaret.

3

DR. MARIAN CHESTER
The Hospital

No, Francis, I haven't much to report. She hasn't spoken since you brought her in. She isn't catatonic, but she is near it, far away in some intense inner life that doesn't touch this one at all. However, there seems to be an innate gentleness in her, a desire to be accommodating, to please, that forces her to get up, to walk about, to eat when she is called. And twice I have found her standing by the window, crying . . . not sobbing, just tears slowly sliding down her cheeks.

Why are you so deeply interested in this case, Frank? It seems unlike you. You always struck me as beautifully detached in your work. But with this patient . . .

Well, I gave her a thorough physical. Everything. She is healthy. Undernourished, but that seems to have been recently. No blemishes or signs of accident, or severe illness of any sort. General condition shows a woman of about twenty-five years of age. Very good teeth. Has had an appendectomy. Oh yes, well, she has had at least one child.

That's all I can tell you at present.

She rouses now and then and tries to help out with the other patients. When they ask her name . . . a few of them do . . . she just says, "Margaret."

4

DR. JOEL GREENBERG

I suppose it is irregular, but you are paying the fees. The management can't object. She is evidently schizophrenic. I don't know much about saints, but I do know something about psychotics, and you have taken on a tough job.

Our field is always vulnerable to attacks, however—and you know this as well as I do, Frank—from families, or from persons who claim they have been railroaded into an asylum or kept there against their will, long after they were able to function in the real world. It is to our advantage to find out about this woman, who she really is and why she is sick, as fast as we can.

Well, I understand that you can't give more than a day a week to it. But couldn't you . . . don't you know anybody who might search the newspapers for a disappearance, or something? Or the police? Oh, well, I see. Yes, of course she is incompetent, couldn't possibly stand trial or anything like that. But we can't harbor a criminal either . . . don't get sore! She could be outside the law, you know.

Frank, you are getting in too deep with this woman. You are allowing yourself to become personally involved, and that just can't be. It affects your work and your competence. I feel obliged to warn you. That will be all, for now.

5

MRS. SULLIVAN
San Francisco

Francis is worried. I feel it. I know it. On his last day off, he scarcely spoke to me, and he only picked at his food. Perhaps the head of Seabright has criticized him for his interest in this girl Margaret. He has many patients there, but Margaret is the only one he talks about.

He is in love with her.

I want to see this girl. This Margaret.

PART II

1

Francis bought a small journal and began keeping notes, for himself. Because of heavy duties at Seabright, he could not be with Margaret as often as he wished. His notes could be read over and added to, slightly changed, as he thought about her. The small notebook was always in his pocket, to refresh his impressions.

"I think she would like to visit a Catholic church," he wrote one day. "We have a small chapel, nondenominational, here in the hospital, and I took her there. She knelt, she seemed to pray, but then she looked about, with undisguised longing. She turned those wonderful eyes toward me, and seemed to be pleading.

" 'Yes?' I encouraged. But she would not answer."

A few days later, he wrote.

"I took her paper and pencils today, plus crayons, in color. She seemed very happy to have them, and smiled her thanks, but up to now, two days later, she hasn't used them, or written anything. The nurses on the floor of the Women's Ward say she has spent less time with the patients, and more sitting quietly, looking out of the window. I went to the window, and there, far off, is a glimpse of the sea, a little sparkle of blue. I wonder if this has any significance."

There followed in his notes some comments on her blood pressure, weight, and general health. For several days, he wrote only, "No change."

The days rolled away, through sunlit noons into the darkness of evening, and Francis was entitled to his day off once more. He had skipped one, for he did not want Dr. Greenberg to decide that he was giving his private patient too much attention, and he ostentatiously stayed over, giving Tomlinson an extra day, and working twenty hours himself. When his own turn came again, he wanted to take the full day, not just the hours after lunch, and he also asked permission to take Margaret out with him.

Dr. Greenberg looked at him quizzically.

"I can't say a thing against you, Frank," he pronounced. "You are careful, dedicated, studious. And you are a good man. I think this is important in our profession, more than in any other. But you've got me worried, I'll admit it."

"You mean my interest in this patient Margaret. Have there been complaints about my attitudes from the other doctors?" asked Francis stiffly.

Dr. Greenberg looked at Frank, and saw only a troubled young man. He was very fond of the youngest appointee to his staff.

"I'm not sure you are really impersonal about this, Frank. I'm not sure I ought to let you keep her here."

"I'll get her admitted somewhere else, if you so direct me," answered Francis stiffly.

Dr. Greenberg studied the young man, the blond hair that stood up in a rough cowlick at the back of his head, the narrow, bright blue eyes behind the glasses. He saw, in different muscle, skin, and hair, himself twenty years before. He too had had an obsession to cure a difficult case, and had bent all his energy to it. Uselessly. Dr. Greenberg's patient had died, raving.

"No. We'll see . . ." murmured Dr. Greenberg. "Maybe . . ." He purposely let his voice trail away. "Have you noticed any improvement at all? Has she spoken?"

"Not to me," answered Francis. "She talks to herself, sometimes. But I have never been able to catch any words."

"In English?"

"I think so. But sometimes in what I think is Italian."

"Hmm. Well. Lots of Italians in San Francisco. Well, okay," he said briskly, suddenly. "Take her to her old haunts. Maybe something will jar loose."

"Thank you."

A few minutes later Dr. Greenberg saw them leave. Dr. Sullivan limped along beside the figure of Margaret, who was wearing a plain cotton dress, with a hospital sweater. Her hair, thick and waving, hung down her back in a heavy dark glossy mane. She was slender and graceful, not tall, just a few inches shorter than Dr. Sullivan.

"Poor kid," murmured Dr. Greenberg. And then, "Poor kids." He sat at his desk, looking into space. Dr. Hirsch came in, having just taken a coffee break, and stopped to smoke a cigarette with Dr. Greenberg.

"One trouble with our job is that we never meet any normal women," commented Greenberg.

"Are there any?" quipped Hirsch. "Can't recall ever having met any. That's why I feel so at home here in the loony bin."

"Why haven't you married? You're old enough."

For once Hirsch was serious.

"I think most women are afraid of psychiatrists," he said. "They think we are mind readers. Nothing a woman resents more."

"Yeah. Maybe." Dr. Greenberg's wife had been difficult the night before.

"Most doctors have trouble with jealousy in their wives," he commented. "I do. But you'd think they wouldn't. Take Sullivan's prize patient. Who could be jealous of a girl that doesn't say anything, seems to have no mother, is obedient and docile?"

Hirsch laughed.

"They hate the docile ones, because men like them," he answered.

2

Margaret demurely took her seat in Francis's little car, and looked around with interest as they rode through the leafy countryside. It was ten in the morning, still fresh-smelling from the cool night.

Francis did not take the direct route home. He had an errand. Presently he took a side road, and after going a few miles, drove through a large gate, where a sign hung which proclaimed "Halsey Kennels." A sound of barking greeted them as he stopped the car. Margaret's face wore a look of expectation.

He got out, went around and opened the door for her. She placed her hand on his arm, and descended with the aplomb of a woman who is used to having doors opened for her. She took his arm with a gesture both gentle and easy.

"I thought you would like to see the dogs," Francis told her, and they walked toward the sounds of baying, yapping, and barking. Mrs. Halsey, the breeder, came forward to meet them.

"Good morning, Doctor. I have chosen a couple of dogs for you to see, according to what you told me on the phone. Come this way."

A trainer was parading two dogs, on leash, in the showing compound. One was a large German shepherd, golden, with dark markings, a male. The other was a golden Irish setter, a bitch.

Margaret went straight to the setter, knelt, and put her arms around the animal's neck, and laid her face against it.

Mrs. Halsey looked. "I guess she has chosen," she said. "That's a fine dog. About a year and two months old. Trained for obedience. And she's affectionate."

The dog seemed to respond warmly to Margaret, twisting about in order to shower kisses on Margaret's forehead and hair.

"That's enough! Sit!" ordered Mrs. Halsey, and the setter immediately sat, trembling with eagerness to be up and moving, but instantly obedient.

"What shall we call your dog, Margaret?" asked the doctor, as she took the setter's leash and put it into her hands.

"Gemma," she answered at once.

"I'll send you a check," Francis told Mrs. Halsey.

Margaret led Gemma to the car, and the dog got in with her, and sat quietly. Francis drove back slowly toward the main highway.

"We are going to my house," he said, "to have lunch with my mother."

There was no answer and Francis felt a stiffness in Margaret, but she made no demur.

Mrs. Sullivan had made arrangements as Francis had asked her to do. "Nobody else, Ma," he had said, over the telephone.

"I see," said Mrs. Sullivan. "You want to see if table manners, how she acts toward a hostess, and so on, can give any clues. Is that it?"

"Something like that."

"Home lunch. Or fancy?"

"Let's not scare her, Ma. A nice family lunch. You be pretty, wear a nice dress, but also an apron. Okay?"

"You want to see if she takes me for a servant or not?"

"Ma, what would I do without you?"

Mrs. Sullivan had set the table simply, with yellow place mats, and heavy dishes she had bought years before from a friend who had taken up ceramics. The dishes were green, with a border in yellow. Instead of a center-piece there was a platter of fruit.

When she heard her son's key in the front door, Mrs. Sullivan went toward him and his guest. She was wearing a flowered apron over her blue dress.

She put out her hand toward the slender woman, whom Francis gently led forward.

"You must be Margaret," said Mary Sullivan. "You are welcome."

Margaret put her hand in Mary's, but gave no answering pressure. She looked grave, but not afraid.

"Frankie, you can put your dog in the back yard, and I'll give it some food later."

Margaret looked worried, but permitted the leash to be taken from her hand, and Gemma was led out through the rooms in the back.

Mary Sullivan urged Margaret gently toward a door.

"Powder room in there," she said, and vanished toward the kitchen. Margaret was left alone. She was emerging when Francis returned. He noted that she had smoothed back her hair, somewhat disordered from the drive, and had left her baggy sweater on a chair.

Mrs. Sullivan came hurrying in with a bubbling casse-role, and called, "Come to the table while it is hot! I hope you like curry, Margaret."

The food was delicious, for Mary was a good cook. She

had thoughtfully provided dishes that were easy to eat, requiring no special manipulation.

Margaret ate daintily, with appetite, as well as with impeccable manners. She smiled at Francis, and then at Mary. Mother and son spoke easily together, about Seabright, about his father and brother, his brother's new girl.

"Is she Catholic, Ma?" asked Francis, Margaret stopped eating and waited for the answer. "Catholic like us, I mean?"

"No, Frankie. She is charming, a little older than Martin, and a divorcee."

"Do you think he will marry her?"

"I think he would like to."

Margaret put down her fork, and her face seemed suffused with sadness, as if the talk of marriage had reminded her of tragedy.

"Would you oppose the marriage?"

"Frankie, I would be sorry, in some ways, but if she truly loves Martin . . . Of course, that remains to be seen. I don't really know yet. She seems to."

Margaret quietly laid her knife and fork side by side on her plate.

As Mary rose to clear the table before bringing in coffee, Margaret gently pressed her back into her chair, and took the three plates herself. She carried them carefully into the kitchen, and returned with the tray on which Mary had laid out the sugar and cream. Mary went to bring the dessert, a chocolate cake she had made and iced that morning.

Margaret sat very still as coffee was served, and accepted her slice of cake, but then she sat staring at it, and slow tears began to course down her checks. Eyes brim-

31

ming, she then rose and left the table. She ran into the powder room, and they heard her there, sobbing.

"What did I do, Frank?" Mary was distressed.

"I don't know. Something surfaced and reminded her of some time in the past that she has blocked out, I would say. Don't worry, Ma. It is probably a good thing. One always wants to open up these closed wounds; they have to bleed, so to speak, before they can heal."

He wrote up the incident carefully in his journal, late that night at Seabright. The ride back had been uneventful, though Margaret had wept afresh at leaving Gemma. Francis had explained that the dog was hers, it was only being cared for her by his mother. Margaret had wanted to take it with her and keep it at Seabright. Francis had explained very carefully why this couldn't be done.

At last she had quieted, had composed herself with an effort, and had followed him obediently out to the car. But she did not speak on the ride back to the hospital, and for some days afterward was very remote and silent. She went back to scrubbing floors and taking on any dirty job that came up, and sometimes had to be forcibly restrained from seizing buckets of slop or mop water.

"A tiny piece in this puzzle," he wrote in his journal. "Might be important, though."

One day, about two weeks later, he found that Margaret had used the crayons to draw a recognizable picture of Gemma, and when he looked at it, she smiled faintly, and raised her dark eyebrows in a question.

"If you like, we can go to visit again soon," he said, "and you may take Gemma for a walk."

The look of radiance that spread over her face haunted him for hours. Such a little thing, so little offered to cause such joy.

3

MRS. SULLIVAN

I searched carefully, Frank. I went every afternoon for
a week, all but one day. I had to do the flowers for the
altar on the Friday, and couldn't then. But I can't find a
thing about any accident or any strange story that involved some young woman. San Francisco papers would
have carried news of anything odd from other California
towns, as well. She seems to have dropped from the sky,
as you say.

4

DR. JOHN TOMLINSON
The Hospital

We're wasting time, Frank. Why don't we use hypnosis
and find out where this woman belongs, and get in touch
with her people? The Chief has suggested it.

Well, yes, under hypnosis she might reveal some deep
trauma that we could begin to treat. I could keep her
under just a short while at a time. Don't think it could
hurt her at all. I won't use medication for inducing a
trance.

I really think, at this point, that we are obliged to do
something practical about finding out who's responsible
for her.

Yes, all right, then. Tomorrow.

DR. TOMLINSON

My God, Frank, she's speaking some foreign language.

DR. SULLIVAN

It's Italian. We'll have to get an interpreter. Bring her out of it now, John.

5
DR. LUIGI PATRONI
Professor of Romance Languages

"Is she ready?"

"Yes."

"She's speaking old Italian. A few words. No. Now she has slipped into modern Italian. I can take this down. I'll have one of my students translate it into English, and I'll send you the transcript.

"Wait . . . she has slipped into English. Apparently she thinks in both languages. I believe you can keep her to English most of the time. If a few words in Italian slip in, I can translate them for you, see where they fit. Yes."

6
MARGARET
In Trance

The grapes are ready. I was working among the vines when he came by. Such a moment! I could smell the dust, the leaves, the crushed grapes my fingers had broken in the picking. And my own sweat, which trickled down from each side of my forehead, despite the red silk scarf I had bound around my hair. I was singing as I worked.

He was riding, but he pulled up his horse, and it snorted and snuffled and pawed the earth. I could smell it, too, the warm horsey smell. Every single moment hangs in my mind, like a golden grape. We were all in strong sunlight; almost it seemed to wrap itself around us, like fur.

I could see that he was not tall, but slim and graceful. Such handsome shoulders, in the gray and rose doublet. One fine leg wore a gray silk stocking, the other was rose. On his tumbled golden curls was a little rose-colored velvet cap, with one long feather.

Marco!

(Here she broke into tears and could not be comforted for some time.)

He asked me my name, and I told him.

"So you live here in Laviano? Why have I never seen you before? I would have remembered."

"My father has the farm there just below. I am not allowed to go anywhere but to church. My father is very strict. But I have to help get in the grapes at harvesttime."

"Margherita."

He stood looking at me, and I felt his eyes like two blue arrows, piercing me. His face was sunburned, but with pink showing through, like a peach. His chin was cleft, and his smile flashed as bright as a knife in the sun, and I saw that his teeth were square and even.

"You are beautiful, Margherita."

"Please go away. My father will punish me if he sees me listening to you."

Two other horsemen came up; they seemed to be friends of Marco. They wore a sort of livery, but also in rose and gray. I supposed Marco must be rich, to have followers.

"Goodbye, Margherita. I will return!"

The three rode away, leaving me in a little cloud of dust which began to settle softly on my old blue gown with the red overskirt that I had looped away from my knees. I went on picking grapes, with trembling fingers. I could still hear his voice, still smell his horse, still see him, still feel the turbulence in my bosom.

I was happy, but I was frightened. Perhaps, I thought, he was only jesting. He won't come back.

But he did. Just before sundown. He was alone. He leaped down from his horse, and stood beside it, the reins loose in his left hand. In the right hand, he held a small package. He took my hand away from the grapes, all stained and dusty as it was, and put the package into it.

"Please, I cannot! What is it?"

"Earrings, for you!"

"Take them back."

"No. You must keep them. You must remember me by them until I can come again. I am from Montepulciano."

I turned, and I looked straight into those bright blue eyes.

"You are the young Lord of Montepulciano."

He smiled.

"So they call me. To you, I am Marco."

"Please leave."

I thrust the package back into his hand. I would not look at him. When he took my chin in his hand and turned my face, I kept my eyes closed. It was then he kissed me. I had never felt any man's lips on mine, never. Father only kissed my brow. Marco's lips were smooth and warm. I felt a warmth and sweetness flood through me, like a draught of wine. *Dio mio!* What will happen to me? I thought.

7

DR. FRANCIS SULLIVAN'S JOURNAL

I had Tomlinson bring her out of the trance too soon, I suppose. What she was telling wasn't to the point. What I want is to find out who she is and where she belongs.

We will let her rest a few days and then do it again.

8

DR. MARIAN CHESTER
A Letter to Her Sister in Oregon

I can't bear it, Sis. First, I shouldn't ever have fallen in love with him. He's younger than I. And he's not handsome, he's short, freckled, wears glasses, and he limps. Some childhood trouble. But I did, I fell bump, bang, in love! I thought, We have our work in common. I set myself to interest him. I tried.

37

But it's hopeless. He is obsessed by a sick Italian girl he found. She thinks she is some medieval saint—and he's engrossed in her case. If I didn't think him so intelligent, such a good doctor, I'd think he was in love with her . . .

9

MARGARET

In Trance

I cried so much, in the days after Marco kissed me. Partly I was afraid of my feelings; I felt as if I were made of honey, all of me, all my body. I kept thinking I was going to melt into a pool of sweetness. Just the thought of him, the taste of his mouth . . .

But mostly I was afraid of my father.

I didn't say a word, of course, and in a way I hoped Marco couldn't come back, because my father and my older brother Cesare would challenge him, perhaps even fight him. And yet I longed to see Marco again.

It was my mother who read in my face that something had happened to me. Mammina! You wouldn't have told Father! It slipped out, I think, because you always were a chatterbox; I think now that you were afraid of Father too, that must be why you always talked so fast and nervously whenever his thick shadow fell across the floor from the open doorway.

He came in to ask why I wasn't out with my basket, getting in the grapes, and Mammina answered, "Oh, she is slow about everything lately. Mooning about like a girl in love."

I suppose he set Cesare to spy on me then, but he was

very sly and careful about it, because I never saw him as I went down the rows with my baskets, filling them, and taking them to the carts. But some of the other workers must have seen Marco come, just at dusk, and stop near where I was working. Perhaps they told him. He said five words, and then Marco rode on toward the town.

"In church, tomorrow, at six," he had said, and I only nodded.

But when it grew dark and I went home, Father seized me, and dragged me to the wine cellar and beat me. Father kept shouting that I was a slut and a hussy, and he would have no brats brought home for him to feed, and who was the man? The pain was terrible, he had wrenched away my blouse, and beat me on my bare back till the blood came, but I didn't answer. What could I say? I had seen him beat some of the young people who helped pick the grapes, and when he was in a rage, he never listened to anyone or stopped yelling himself. Was he perhaps a little mad? I suppose so now, though at that time, I was only fifteen, I just thought all fathers were this way.

After he was tired, I lay on the floor there, unable to get up or go to my bed, and nobody came to help me or wash me. My mother didn't dare. I stayed there all night, trying to sleep, trying to think what to do. I knew I could not go to the church at six; I couldn't go anywhere. And I was terrified that Marco might come again to look for me, and that my father would catch him and kill him.

But in the night, in the darkness and in pain, I began to perceive how I might save Marco from my father's fury.

In the morning, I managed to drag myself out to the water buckets, where I washed myself and mopped away

39

some of the blood from my back. I went inside, where my mother was setting out bread and wine for breakfast. She came to me then, and helped me, put some salve on my hurts and covered them with cotton cloth, and brought me a clean blouse.

"I have done no wrong, Mammina," I told her. "The man who spoke to me is the young Lord of Montepulciano, an important personage. Is one to answer him discourteously?"

That is all I said, knowing my mother would tell it at once to my father. And Father was always very obsequious with the rich lords of the town. I had remembered how he smiled and bowed and tried to be pleasant, when he went to take wine for his tax, and when he tried to sell extra skins of new wine for the lords' tables. He had never been to Montepulciano, but in Laviano, and in Cortona, he often went to beg audience with the great signores.

I was at peace then for many days. My back healed, and Father, though he did not speak to me, did not beat me again. Of course I was not at Church when Marco had waited for me, and he did not come anymore to the vineyard. So rich and so handsome, and a lord as well, he could have any one of dozens of girls, I knew. I had failed him; he would forget me as easily as he might change the feather in his cap.

10

DR. CHESTER
The Hospital

I am not sure you ought to go on, Frank. She cries and trembles for hours after each session. And what have you learned? Only that she has some very deeply entrenched obsession. I'd say let her alone. She may come back to reality by herself.

11
DR. GREENBERG

Frank, I've been reading the transcripts made when you subjected this woman, this Margaret, to hypnosis. I don't know what to make of them. She doesn't sound mad to me. She sounds possessed. If I believed at all in these things, I'd think she had somehow got into the wrong time plane, or that the original Margaret she seems to think she is got ejected from her own century, somehow, into ours. But what good does this do us? We can only speculate and marvel. We haven't found out anything whatsoever about this woman herself, where she belongs, who she is. I think I'll have to ask you to stop the trance sessions. Try rest and medication. Simple tranquilizers and nourishing food for a while. Let her alone.

12
DR. LOUIS MICHELLOD
Professor of Medieval History

Yes, what can I do for you?

No. I have never come across anything of the sort. My field is history, early Middle Ages, but I haven't ever had anything to do with hagiography beyond the fact of the existence of saints and religious orders. And of course, a much more pervasive religious outlook on life, among the

41

people, than now. But, this patient must be very much of a challenge. I'd be glad to study the transcripts if you want me to. Not that I feel I could contribute anything. Except authenticity, perhaps. But then, you must bear in mind, that even the authenticity of a historian is based on documents and reports, and it cannot be looked upon as a final authority in any way. Oh, I could catch some obviously modern note . . . some faux pas. I mean, I think I could tell at once if this woman is a fake.

13
DR. ANANDA GUPTA LAL
Hindu Teacher, Oakland

My good sir, I fear you consider me a sort of charlatan, an impostor. Otherwise, why subject me to such tests? Ah, of course, as you explain it, that is another matter. Certainly I believe in the transmigration of souls. In some unusual cases, it seems that the soul progresses into another life fully dressed, you might say, in all personality, history, and tastes of the individual in the former life. Happily for most of us, we arrive in a new envelope of flesh with almost no memory of the past. I say *almost* because, in some cases . . . involving very sensitive persons . . . part of the past can be recovered, in a flash of recognition, or a sort of vision.

Yes, I understand.

I could not tell you anything at all without seeing the person you speak of. Speaking with her I might learn something about her present incarnation. I could surmise something of past sojourns here on this planet.

And I might not. I promise nothing. I obligate myself to nothing.

Also remember please, I am a busy person. Occupied. I teach religion here in this humble school, and I have many disciples.

14
DR. SULLIVAN
San Francisco

Gentlemen, I have asked you here, to my home, to conduct an investigation that I find is outside the field of medicine. My chief at the hospital has forbidden me to subject the patient to any more hypnotic trances, but after much careful thought and consultation with various experts in a number of fields, I think it would be valuable to do so, quite apart from the hospital and without involving it in any way in the possible results of this study.

The patient is a young woman who seems to have no connections of any kind with persons or things in this life; that is, she suffers from a peculiar sort of amnesia, in that she has substituted another life, complete with family, home, and sentiments, for what must have been her own. I say "what must have been" because the substitute life she seems to have taken as her own is that of an obscure saint of the early Middle Ages, known to us as Margaret of Cortona.

We have had no success whatever in learning anything of the actual life and connections of this patient, despite several sessions of hypnotic trance, during which, in every instance, she seems to have retreated completely into the personality of Margaret of Cortona.

Dr. Michellod is an expert on medieval studies; Dr. Gupta Lal is a learned Hindu who teaches and believes in the reincarnation of souls. Dr. Tomlinson is an expert in the hypnotic management of patients.

I regard this patient as peculiarly mine. Her case interests me profoundly.

So we will slide her into a trance again and each one of us will be alert to any sort of clue that might lead to learning more about her, or to how she might be helped.

15

MARGARET

In Trance

It was such a beautiful day. The harvests were in, and I hadn't much to do. Winter was coming, but I felt only the golden warmth of the sun, smelled the dry sweet fragrance of the corn shocks. My father let the cows into the harvested fields, to eat the short dry stubble that was left; I had a long switch to guide them with, though the old belled cow who led our little herd was docile and good, and minded my voice.

And then he came, riding on his horse. Marco. He didn't greet me, or call my name. He simply leaned down, took me by the waist and lifted me up so that I sat on the horse, just behind him.

"Put your arms around my waist, hang on!" he said, and he struck his steed a blow. I felt the animal gather its legs for a leap and we set off across the fields, jumping over the little stone fences, as fast as flying! Marco's back was so broad, his neck so strong, his head set so firmly on his shoulders! When he turned his head, the shape of his eyelids, the curve of his nostril, the lifted line of his lips in profile, were beautiful. I perceived the beauty of masculinity, of men, as I had never thought of it with regard to my father or my brother Cesare.

I lost track of time, in that flying over the fields with Marco. He stopped, beneath a tree that still held enough leaves to give some shade, leaped down, and held up his arms to me. And I went into them, and there I stayed.

The leaves above us, as we lay, were gold and red, from the first frosts. With patches of deep blue sky between, and the swiftly moving white clouds, it was a pattern of loveliness to watch, as my body learned of another beauty, heart-stopping, ecstatic. Ah, but I should not call back and remember those moments of joy, I should not!

(Here she broke into tears, sobbing and heaving herself about. Dr. Tomlinson, after a few moments, decided to release her from the trance.)

16
MRS. SULLIVAN

Margaret is to stay with me. She is very tired. Frank, will you take the gentlemen into the dining room? I have left some coffee and cake there for you. I will put Margaret to bed.

17
JOHN WADE

Mrs. Sullivan? Yes. John Wade here. I just wanted to tell you that this girl Margaret, who comes to help out sometimes, has come back. She says she is staying with you. Yes, sure, she is talking. Why? Was there . . . ? Oh, I see. No, she seems just as always to us, and she is very helpful. Oh, here she is. She says to tell you she will come back this evening, if she may. Yes, I'll tell her. Goodbye.

18
MRS. SULLIVAN

Of course you are the doctor, Frank, and I shouldn't presume to tell you what to do. But Margaret seems to me to be useful and happy doing what she does. She works at the mission, she goes to church and prays, she takes Gemma for walks. How she loves that dog! She does kind little things for me, errands, looks after my comfort. Why not just let her be? Or, if you think it's your duty, why don't you just put a few words in the paper. You know? Somebody might come forward who knows something about her. Oh.

19
DR. GUPTA LAL

Yes, Dr. Sullivan, I found the session I attended and the transcripts I read extremely interesting. The young woman herself, also. It was an unfinished incarnation, I believe. Interrupted, somehow, she . . . in this time plane . . . has not finished what she began there, in the previous life, and it oppresses her. The former demands that she finish some task begun. This is my diagnosis. Not a medical one, Doctor. It is a strong perception I received, although I do not know any more about this Margaret than I heard. You will think me a romantic, in spite of my beard and my white hairs. But this young woman experienced some profound love, I would say, that must be culminated here. Perhaps she was a suicide in some former life. There was an aura of joy around her, as she spoke at your house, but I saw swirling clouds of tragedy around her, too.

Yes, if you wish, I could return her to that previous life, and learn more of her. If I may permit myself to say so, I am much subtler, less dependent on drugs, and can take the person deeper into a remembered life, than your so scientific Dr. Tomlinson. I am from a very ancient race, and we knew arts and methods in dealing with time that the West has only begun to perceive. But forgive. You will think me a braggart, a poseur. Nevertheless, I affirm that my method would do your young lady less harm than these drug-induced sessions. Yes, I said "your" young lady. She is yours, is she not?

20
SAN FRANCISCO *EXAMINER*
April 3, 1927

Any person having knowledge of the disappearance of a young woman, approximately twenty-five years old, dark waving hair, gray eyes, about five feet four, weight 112 pounds, please communicate with Dr. Francis Sullivan, Box 855, care of this newspaper.

21
SAN FRANCISCO *EXAMINER*
May 4, 1927

Any person having any knowledge of the young woman calling herself Margaret of Cortona, who works among the poor in South San Francisco, please communicate with Dr. Francis Sullivan, Box 855, care of this newspaper.

22
MRS. SULLIVAN

No, everything is the same, Frank. Exactly the same. She is gentle and good, works all the time, doing whatever seems at hand, things I couldn't . . . well, I admit it, I wouldn't do . . . among those people. Sometimes she is away for days and comes back here, back home, I like to think, weary and dirty. Then she washes herself and her clothes, and sleeps and eats a little. She is getting too thin. She is courteous, even affectionate. She talks about the people she helps.

23
DR. GREENBERG
The Hospital

Well, there being no unusual cases to discuss, everything being under control, as the young folks say, I propose to make a speech. A speech and a prophecy. We are here, Doctors, working in a new branch of our discipline, trying to induce, provoke, or perhaps merely observe changes for the better in our patients. Sometimes we do, sometimes we don't. Changes in their behavior and attitudes sometimes occur, for better or worse, due to no cause we can identify. The head of a mental hospital in Texas, a state-endowed hospital, has the greatest number of patients released of any hospital in the country. Why? Perhaps his diagnoses are more lenient than ours. Or perhaps what he claims is a contributing factor has validity; he says it is contact with the earth. He puts all his patients, even the catatonics, out onto land, to work on it, or at least, to sit on it. Sounds like old wives' tales and so on. But not all the old wives were fools, let's admit. May be something in it.

Now for my prophecy. I am here as chief of a hospital, and I am running this institution to the best of my ability. But I believe the day is coming when we won't have any institutions like ours. I believe . . . I truly hope . . . the day is coming, when we will find some ways to get people well enough to function in the real world, whether they are crazy or not. Because we are all a little crazy.

Look at Frank, there. Solemn as a judge, responsible, devoted to his cases, an excellent doctor, studious, kind, helpful. But once outside these walls, on his day off, he moons around a poor woman who thinks she is living in some past age, and he can't do a thing about her. So who's crazy?

And Tomlinson there, with his test tubes and boxes of pills. Tom, what would you do if I asked you to throw them all down the toilet? I'd have to straitjacket you.

Dr. Chester, what is a pretty woman like you doing around here, bothering with senile old women and

49

bitches like that Morissey woman, when you ought to be cooking for a husband and three kids? And you, Hirsch, well . . . No, I guess I'll let you and Phillips off. I'll take up your psychoanalysis at a later session. My wife has planned another state dinner, with crowns and robes. Ha! If I'm late again she'll skin me.

24

DR. SULLIVAN'S JOURNAL
July 20, 1927

I seem to have made no progress whatsoever with Margaret's case. But an orderly account of what has been done may be helpful eventually, if she is ever brought back into the present real world where she functions successfully but in a very limited manner. This case history may prove of some historical value.

First. She is Catholic. Perhaps of Latin blood, since so few Anglo-Saxon Catholics even know about Margaret of Cortona. Of course, we have a large Italian community as part of San Francisco.

In appearance, she is a rather unusual type. Probably meant to be full-figured, though, because of limited food, she is very slender. But the hips are wide, the bosom deep. A very womanly type. Her face is not beautiful by modern standards, I suppose; I judge by the movies and by the pictures of models in magazines. Margaret's face is oval, leading from a broad brow and large deep eyes to a small mouth and gentle chin. Her mouth is not full-lipped, but delicately curved; the teeth are rather small and not perfectly even. Yet she has a tender, lovely smile, with lips closed, more like the faces of medieval Virgins than of any modern girl. Her nose is slender, well formed, but somewhat long by modern standards, which seem to prefer the snub nose. I understand that some women even go and have operations to shorten their noses. Irrelevant comment. Her hands, despite the hard work she has been doing, are well formed, with long, slender fingers. The nails are short, and the fingers and palm firm and muscled; I might think she has a musician's hands, but have not been able to establish any connection here. Most impressive are her eyes. They are very large, with lids that curve around the eyeball, marking the eye socket. In color, they are a strange, shining light gray, the iris surrounded by a slender darker line, and they are shaded by long, dark lashes that curve upward. Her eyebrows are curved, rather thick. And her hair, which she keeps covered with a dark silk scarf, is a dark brown, and wavy.

To me, she seems very beautiful, but not all the doctors think so.

As for her behavior at the hospital, although she went along with me willingly enough, and when there began at once to try to look after the other patients in the Women's Ward, she ceased communicating. Several of my colleagues questioned her, but she would answer only Yes or No to necessary questions. There was no evidence of any Italian in her speech.

In order to try to find out something about her background, her people, we tried induced hypnosis, twice. Transcripts of what she said are here attached.

August 3   Continued Diary

Attached herewith also are transcripts of comments made, after the sessions of hypnosis, by Dr. Tomlinson,

M.D., Dr. Michellod, an expert in medieval history, and Dr. Gupta Lal, a learned Hindu who lectures on Hinduism, the transmigration of souls, reincarnation, and other mystical matters.

Margaret left the hospital (where I had been paying her fees, an expense I could not continue) and took up residence with my mother at our home in San Francisco. My mother is an intelligent and kind woman, and she became deeply interested in Margaret's case. It was decided among us to allow her to come and go freely, as she wished, and she immediately began to search out and care for the indigent sick and dying, as before. Only now she returns to my mother's house to wash, to eat, and sometimes to sleep. She has not volunteered any information about herself whatsoever. She prays very much, and often spends hours in a church near our home, in deep meditation.

I have the beginning of a theory that she might be startled into recognition of herself as a person, not the reincarnated saint, by the sudden announcement of a sort of Key Word. I have observed several cases in the hospital in which a Key Word seems to provoke or induce a violent reaction in mentally afflicted persons, the word carrying within itself a whole panoply of visions and responses. So far, I have seen this in at least three cases. Reports of those cases may be seen at the hospital. It will be observed that in every case, the Key Word brought forth an access of the hallucination, or the specific mental deviation. Yet I wonder if finding such a Key Word for Margaret might not also induce such a violent reaction that we could harvest some clues from it.

I suppose such a word might have to be sought in Italian as well as in English.

August 8

I have consulted Dr. Guido Parenti, of the University of California, and have briefed him on the case. He was willing to compile a few words for me, in Italian, that might possibly provoke some response.

August 9

I made use of a few of the words Dr. Parenti thought might be useful, but with no special response whatsoever. At *"Dio"* she quite naturally folded her hands in prayer. At *"amore"* she smiled, and even dropped her lids over her eyes, as if in shyness, but that was probably because I was speaking to her, and she has always acted docile, that is, obedient, with me, but otherwise, somewhat reserved.

August 12

There has been nothing in particular to record about Margaret in the last weeks, save that my mother has grown increasingly devoted to her. In fact, my mother has begun to bother me about my attempts to bring Margaret into the real world. "Let her alone," she says in exasperation. "There are too few saints about, she is useful, and happy. What more can anyone want of life?" I explain that at any time Margaret's illness, or hallucinations, may take another turn, bring her into trouble or tragedy. But now I question myself. Is it just the case that fascinates me so much? Is it truly a wish to return Margaret to

53

whatever was her place in the world before she took refuge in the personality of this long-gone saint? I don't like my answers.

August 20

On my day off from the hospital, I went home, as usual, and visited my mother, and checked up on Margaret's movements. I keep in touch daily by telephone, but I always try some careful questions, when I see her. I was startled, yesterday, after supper—a meal which Margaret came hastily in from the street to share with us—to notice that she seems to have moments of sudden drowsiness, or even sleep. It could be petit mal, or evidence of some other physical trouble. But in one of those moments, relaxed, in the darkening living room after supper, it seemed to me that she fell naturally into the trance that had been drug-induced before. She did not say anything intelligible, and in fact seemed to be murmuring in Italian, and she squirmed and grimaced as if in great pain. She came out of this spontaneously, and seemed startled, even afraid, of me. I put my hand on her arm, and she began to tremble uncontrollably. But then suddenly she recognized me . . . I saw recognition in her eyes . . . and she sighed and smiled. Shortly after, she said good night, and I heard her telling my mother that she would go to bed and get a good sleep, for she intended to rise very early and go to take care of an elderly invalid in South San Francisco who would be waiting for her.

I got in touch with Gupta Lal, who confirmed what I suspected, that Margaret might at any time fall into the hypnotic trance herself. This poses some troublesome problems. Should it happen somewhere away from my home, or someplace where she is not safe, she could be in danger.

Gupta Lal says I should let him induce deep hypnosis once more, and try to clear away whatever emotions or "memories" (as he calls them) tug her mind.

I have to think this through. I certainly don't want to do her any harm. And, as my mother says, she is a saint. Why change her?

September 2

Dr. Gupta Lal came to our house, my mother's house, and with almost no trouble at all, he sent Margaret into a deep trance. She sighed, as a person does who has tried to sleep, and has not been able to, and then at last slips into a doze.

Almost at once she began a whispering confidence, as if she were retelling an experience to someone dear. She spoke in English, with only an occasional word in Italian. Herewith follows a transcription, word for word, of my shorthand notes on the session.

25
MARGARET
In Trance

Marco came to find me several times afterward, and I plunged deeper into the joys of love. I had never suspected, never dreamed, that bodies could yield such a harvest of pleasure. Besides the sensations of thrilling, almost painful pleasure, my mind and heart seemed burning with joy to be able to give and yield the treasures of happiness Marco felt and shared with me. How could this be wrong? Had not God made our young bodies for this ecstasy?

We hid under a tall tree with heavy drooping branches that made us a sort of tent against the sky. With Marco's arms around me, I felt safe. Ay! But I wasn't. Cesare spied on us, and he told my father.

So that one day, hurrying home in the still-light evening (my father had sent me to hoe the vegetable patches between some of the vines . . . we grew salad greens there, and onions . . .), I found my father waiting for me, strap in hand.

He dragged me to the cellar and beat me there. It was terrible. I swooned, so I don't know how long it went on. And he locked me in.

I lay in my own blood all that night, and my blouse stuck to the open welts; at the slightest movement, I felt myself bleeding, and the pain was intense.

In the morning someone, perhaps my mother, opened the cellar door and pushed in a cup of water and a piece of dry bread, but I could not eat. I drank a little water and patted some on my forehead, and lay in my misery, I don't know how long.

The shadows that lengthened during the day, as I slipped into a sort of sleep, showed me the hours that fled. There was no lessening of the pain. What a punishment! To be punished for love! Surely this was not God's plan!

Night fell, and all was quiet; I heard no more steps passing to and fro above me. Everyone had gone to sleep.

I had no idea of the hour when there was a soft cutting sound, but I could see nothing in the dark. Marco had come. He had drugged the dogs with some chemical in the meat he threw them, and he had four of his men with him, in case anyone awoke. But he was soft and silent. It was Marco who sawed through the cellar door, gently, quietly, and then at last opened it. He came to me and lifted me in his arms. I knew that I must be silent, but oh, I could not. I cried out, and groaned, as his arms pressed against my wounds. At once I heard stirrings above. We stayed quiet, unmoving, and the sounds above subsided. Marco's horses were tethered some distance away, but the noise of their restless hooves might seem to come from our own stables.

So quietly, Marco supporting me, we made our way around the house to where his men waited. There was only a sliver of moon, and there were scudding clouds, as well, to make any moving shadow seem to be part of the uneasy night.

Marco lifted me onto his mount; I bit my lips to keep from crying with the pain, and when at last we reached a small stone house on his lands, where he let me down, I had bitten them through. How horrible I must have looked to him, as the dawn came up, with my blouse matted and stuck to my back, my hair in disarray, my face streaked with tears and blood.

He held me, so gently, and I saw that he was pale, and his lips trembled.

"My poor little love," he murmured brokenly. "*Poverina, poverina, poverina del mio cuore . . .*"

When I could look around, I saw that there was another man, besides the four men wearing swords and daggers that Marco had brought with him. This personage was tall, white-haired, and thin, wearing a long dark gown to his heels.

"This is Messer Hilario, a learned doctor. He will cure you . . . oh, it won't hurt . . . you will drink some spiced wine first, to make you sleep, and when you waken, you will be better, your wounds dressed. And I will not leave your side. Not for a moment!"

I took the flagon of wine, which tasted both sweet and bitter, and drank it thirstily. Very soon I felt a soft darkness rushing toward me, and then it overwhelmed me, and I knew no more.

When I woke, it was night once more. Outside the little stone house, I heard the trees moaning in a rising wind, and then the first drops of rain began to fall. Soon there was a gentle thrumming sound all around us. I began to feel safe again; Marco's men guarded the door, the night was full of a cloak of rain, and Marco lay asleep beside me, one arm flung across me.

My back burned and ached, but the doctor had bound me with many bandages, so that movement would not hurt so much, and there must have been some unguent too, to help deaden the pain. I slept deeply, and in the morning, when a soft light entered the cottage, I awoke ravenously hungry.

(Here Margaret stirred and stretched herself and sighed. She did not speak for some time, and I thought she would emerge from her trance, but Dr. Gupta Lal signaled me to silence, and waited, passively.)

And then began that time, the years of my happiness. Four years and a few months. Ah, it cannot be evil that I recall that happiness. But of course, it was selfish: I was at the center of a wheel of joy, which revolved around me. Still, I did no harm to anyone. But I must try not to think of that time . . . I must not . . . because of . . ."

(Dr. Gupta Lal spoke, softly and persuasively. "No, it

must be remembered," he said. "Every moment, every word. It must be remembered, and told . . .")

My time of joy. Ah!

At first, Marco stayed with me most of every day, and he came every night. I learned from the guards who watched over me that this small stone house was only one of many that belonged to his tenants, farmers who worked the lands for him. He lived in the palace, higher on the hill, surrounded by parks and gardens.

At first, in my ignorance, and in the peaceful joy of my days and the ecstasies of the nights, I asked no questions. I simply accepted, and blessed God for my safety and my happiness.

Marco brought me lovely clothes to wear. Not the coarse cotton of my blouses, the heavy coarse wool of the skirts I had worn. These dresses were made of wool so thin and fine I could look through it and see the outlines of trees; of delicate fine cotton, transparent as the wing of a dragonfly; velvets in deep glowing colors . . . blue and dark red, and leaf green. He would not let me wear any covering for my hair except bands of silk to hold my heavy locks back from my face. He loved my hair, and wanted it to be free and floating always. I knew that the loose women of the town wore their hair free like this, and the virtuous women covered their heads, as Holy Church demanded. But for me, Marco was my lord. What he wanted I did, and gladly. I washed myself and my hair often; I dried my hair in the sun, and I rubbed olive oil on my hands, to soften them.

There was no news of my father. And I wanted none. I was desperately afraid of him, and I knew myself to have done wrong for which he would never forgive me. My father had protected my virginity because he hoped to

59

marry me well to some old widower who wanted a young
and tender wife, and who would give wide acres and
much gold for one. I believe he even had the man in
mind to whom I was to be given. Or sold, like a fine
heifer. Still, he was my father, the authority over me,
and Padre Bartolomeo at the church had always told me
that the second commandment was Honor thy father
and thy mother.

I used to wonder, shouldn't there be a commandment
Love thy children? But it seems that God did not com-
mand this, and parents did with their children as they
wished.

In my fear of my father, I was terrified one day when
the guard Marco had always at the door for me, or
watching over me if I walked in the garden or picked
poppies in the fields, came and said he had to ride at once
to the palace.

A flag had been put out from the tower, which was the
signal to him to return at once.

I was not a bride, nor even betrothed. I was a mistress,
and could not live in the palace while Marco's father was
the old Lord.

The guard mounted his horse, and rode toward the hill-
side, and I was left alone. I became quite useless with
fear. My knees would not hold me up, my limbs trembled,
and I found that I was making a continuous whimpering
sound. I went distractedly from room to room in the little
stone house, seeking a corner that might be secure, or at
least hidden. There was none, though I barred the door in
the front. But I knew a strong man like my father could
burst through that door. It was dark when Marco came
for me, and he found me cowering in an upper room, gib-
bering with terror.

He comforted me in his arms, and I saw that his dear eyes filled with tears. At last I was persuaded to eat some supper with him (one of his men had bread and wine and some cheese) and sleep. The next day, he brought me Gemma.

I named her Gemma, for the dog was like a jewel in the sun. Her hide was golden, close to her body, and silken to the touch. She had strong hocks and slim legs for swift running, and a great massive jaw, and her eyes were large and beautiful. Gemma was to be with me in everything I did and everywhere I went, to defend me. I came to love her, for her perfect loyalty, her warm and constant affection, and with her near, I began to lose my terror of my father and of Cesare.

Marco told me that his father was feeble, and lay constantly on his bed now, and because of his delicate health, he insisted daily that Marco marry. Marco had been betrothed, years ago, to a younger daughter of one of the lords of Siena, who was now thirteen and of an age to marry.

"And when will you marry?" I asked in a whisper, not allowing myself to think of what might become of me.

"I shall not marry," Marco told me. He swore it on the memory of his mother, and I believed him.

Later I learned that he had so sworn to his father, but that old man would not listen and was sure that Marco, strong and vigorous in his beautiful youth, would surely bring a bride to the castle, one day. So Marco's father grew weaker, and one day in the winter he died.

Marco left me then for all the days of the mourning and the funeral, but also he left men to guard me, and I had Gemma. I waited in what patience I could muster for his return to me.

And he did return. What a joyous reunion! We feasted

and made love, and slept long in the morning, close in each other's arms. Ah, Dio. How happy I was.

Then Marco told me to make bundles of my clothes and the jewels he had given me; I was to live in the palace with him. He could not marry me, being betrothed to the daughter of a great signore, but he intended to put off the marriage day constantly until perhaps the lady would ask to be freed from her promise.

"She will," he told me. "Or they will make her. There are plenty of other matches for her. And as for me, I love only my Margherita, and I will have no other."

The palace was in mourning, but Marco insisted that I go there with him at once. I was obedient, of course, but I managed to keep close to the room where we slept, and when I moved through the halls, or went out for exercise with Gemma, I wore my darkest clothes and a veil. I tried, indeed I tried, to behave discreetly. But of course, time went by, and gradually the servants seemed to accept me, perhaps because Marco demonstrated his love for me so openly, so often. They all adored the young Lord, and as I pleased and amused him, they were willing to accord me their careless affection, too.

Gemma guarded me with all the loyalty and love in her great heart. Her beautiful eyes were on me at all times, except when she drowsed by the fire at my feet, and then she frequently woke from her dreams, to look at me, thump her tail against the floor, and then rest her nose on her paws once more. Sometimes she started up, growling deep in her throat, showing her long white teeth. She saw invisible dangers sometimes, but I trusted her. I never moved from where I stood, when she saw evil in the shadows.

In the spring the weather suddenly softened and then

became warm, and I rummaged in the chests in our room for lighter clothes. To my surprise, the belts would not close around my waist, and I . . . stupid as I had been in my constant daze of love . . . had not counted the moons, or paid any attention to the rhythms of my being except as they answered those of my love. There was an elderly servingwoman who had done my washing and the steaming of my veils, and she saw my look of dismay as I struggled to fasten one of the last summer's gowns. She had always been taciturn, scowling-browed, but now she smiled with delight, and patted me on the arm.

"In about five months' time," she told me, sharing with me woman's delight and awe at the news. A child was forming in my womb, a small person, another soul, a babe for me and Marco. I felt nothing but exhilaration at the thought, and could hardly wait for Marco to come in from the hunt, to tell him.

How long we talked, by a small fire, at a table with cups and wine nearby. I wore a bedgown, loose and flowing, creamy wool, with an overgown of deep blue. He laid his hand, his dear hand, on my belly, where we waited, both of us, to feel the leaping of our child. But it was some weeks more before we felt that tiny flutter, that little ripple of movement.

Before my lying-in, word came from the lord in Siena that his daughter was very young, that young men must have their pleasures, and that he was content to continue to honor the marriage contract he had made with Marco's father. "Let a few years go by, until he tires of his harlot," was the message, and Marco turned white and then red with anger at the words. I felt dismay, and the tug of a cold presentiment at my heart, but my child was growing in my body, and I could not grieve too much at the insult. It was true, I supposed. My father would so name me.

My child was born at dawn of a beautiful June day. His first cry mingled with the first sounds of morning . . . birds awakening, the animals in the stables making their sounds together, the work of the palace beginning in the freshness of the new day. I had had a long labor . . . all the day before, and all the night . . . and toward the end I had wallowed and wailed, all my will to silence and dignity gone. I lay with my hair full of sweat and my nightgown dripping with it, and dirtied with blood, but Maria, the servingwoman who had first told me that I would be a mother, had helped me through all the wrenching pains. She made me walk, and then at last crouch on the birthing stool and hang onto the cords she tied on the back of that chair.

I had not dozed, except fitfully, and I whispered to her that I must be clean, must be pretty, as well as the babe, before Marco came in. She washed the little one, and wrapped him in swaddling clothes, and then sponged me and bound me tightly around the waist, leaving my breasts free. I felt full of pain and bruises, but she managed to slip a fresh gown around me, and then she brushed and dried my hair and made braids with bright ribbons, to lay a bit of color next to my white cheeks.

"Now," I whispered. "Now!" And he flew into the room, dropped to his knees, and embraced us both, our little baby boy and me.

Could anyone on earth be more fortunate than I? Or happier than I? I thought not. My babe sucked, and grew strong, my lover cherished us, we lived in great comfort and ease.

Marco named our child Giovanni, but I think I never

called him anything but *il mio piccolo amore*. My little love. I would have thought, before his birth, that my heart could hold only one love, my overflowing love for Marco, but the heart expands, and the spirit grows larger, and the love grows and encompasses all. Every morning and evening of my life, I knelt to say my prayers and thank God for my happiness.

26
DR. SULLIVAN'S JOURNAL
September 5

I demanded that Dr. Gupta Lal let Margaret rest then, and in a little while she came out of her trance, and seemed at first bewildered, then quite calm.

"Did you learn anything about me?" she asked, almost fearfully.

"Many things," said Dr. Gupta Lal, easily. "But only about your life in times past. Not the present one."

Margaret looked at me, in inquiry.

"I will explain it to you," I answered her, "after you have rested and have had some food."

My mother had given up many of her activities, her bridge games, her movies with other women friends, some community work, in order to help me with Margaret. I thought I could please her and perhaps Margaret by inviting them out to dinner, and I arranged to take them to Chinatown for an evening of exotic pleasures. My mother saw to it that Margaret was dressed reasonably for this excursion, though in the dark unobtrusive clothes she preferred, and my mother took young delight in all the preparations. Gemma was to be fed and left in the kitchen, my mother went and had her hair dressed (Margaret gently refused to do this) and her nails manicured. I bought them each a gardenia from a stand on Grant Avenue, and as I pinned it to Margaret's dark coat, I saw that her eyes were focused on something distant and sad. But she did not say anything. In all things she was promptly and almost disconcertingly obedient, and she did as I instructed her, though she made it plain that she would rather have spent all her time in church at prayer or with her beloved poor and sick. But I thought I must start to break this pattern, and bring around the lodestar of her life toward herself.

Margaret looked around with sudden awakened interest at the dragons and kites and other Chinese symbols with which the restaurant was decorated, and listened with interest while I ordered the meal. When the dishes came, to my astonishment she asked for chopsticks, and when they arrived, she settled them in her fingers correctly, and began to eat with them, as if she had handled them all her life. My mother looked at me, and I at her.

A clue, it seemed, at last!

"You are not using knife and fork," I commented. The scent of the gardenia was sweet around her face, as she leaned forward to answer me.

"It seems so natural to use chopsticks," she answered, faintly.

"But Margaret of Cortona never used them," I said.

She dropped her eyes then, and seemed upset. She started to pick up her knife and fork, but then she set them down again, firmly, and returned to the chopsticks.

"You must find out why I do this," she said. She was agitated and distraught.

66

She was putting all the load of finding out about herself on my shoulders.

"Who am I?" she suddenly asked me.

She ate the Chinese dinner, and afterward, we strolled along the avenue looking into the shopwindows, admiring the jade jewelry. My mother exclaimed and indicated the things she thought most beautiful; she took Margaret into one shop and bought her a Chinese dressing gown. Mother wanted her to have the silk one, but Margaret rejected it firmly, and at last, persuaded, selected one of pale blue cotton, printed with a design of bamboo. It was attractive but cheap, many dollars less in price than the silk gown. Margaret was gentle but adamant.

"I have no right," she kept saying. "No right to your kindness."

Later, I took them to a hall where there was a program of dancing and Chinese acrobats. Among the turns was that of a juggler; he spun plates on sticks, first a couple in his right hand, then two in his left hand. Then lying on the floor he set plates spinning on sticks held between his toes . . . first one, then two, and finally four. It was a remarkable performance, but I was unprepared for Margaret's reaction.

Suddenly she rose, with a choked cry, and ran out of the room. It was not easy to catch her, and I had to leave my mother to pay and to find her way out as best as she could. When at last I caught up with Margaret she was hiccuping and sobbing. But she couldn't or wouldn't say what had upset her.

We went home. The next day my mother phoned me at the hospital to tell me that Margaret had spent the day in church, and would not eat.

I was left to ponder all these items, but I could not find

any enlightenment beyond the obvious fact that she must have visited Chinese restaurants often, often enough to learn to eat with chopsticks, and perhaps may even have seen the same Chinese juggler before. My only clues.

Oh, and two others. She knew Italian.

And there was Gemma.

Despite the importance of Gemma in the visions she recounted as the medieval Margherita, I felt sure there must be some significance from her present life in the presence of the big golden dog, so gentle and protective.

But beyond those three small clues, I was in the dark. But still, only five months had passed. Patience.

27

DR. GREENBERG
The Hospital

Frank, I am satisfied with your work. Your patients seem to respond to you very well, in spite of the relapse of that German woman . . . Mrs. Fetterman? Yes, Fetterman. Well, I find no criticism of your treatment, in any case.

How are you getting along with that extracurricular case of yours? The woman who thinks she is a saint. I read your transcripts, and you know something? I think this Gupta Lal seems as close to the thing as anybody.

As I see it, there is no essential progress made. She insists on doing all this personal charity, she accepts what you and your mother give her, as she might accept a duty from a superior in a convent. Now there's a possibility. Have you considered that she might well have spent some time in a convent? I'm no Catholic, but I believe there are more than a few cases of neurosis among these women that lock themselves up, away from the world. Why don't you check into the convents around the state? There probably are more than a few in which the nuns are Italian, some Italian order, even. There was never any response to your newspaper appeals. Try the convents.

28
DR. MARIAN CHESTER

I'd like to come over to see your patient someday, Frank. She interests me, too. There was something very ladylike —to use an old-fashioned word—about her. Something gentle and, well, good. And your mother must feel somewhat restrained, always waiting for Margaret to appear, always being at the ready, so to speak.

Yes. I could take a few days off, and stay with your mother and Margaret while you make the trip. To visit convents? Oh, but Frank! I could help you there, perhaps, more than being with your mother. I think I would know how to approach the nuns. And some are cloistered, you know. Still, the Mother Superior might talk with me. Oh, let me!

All right. I'll be ready next Wednesday, and we can try a few around San Francisco.

29
DR. SULLIVAN'S JOURNAL
September 20

On the suggestion of my chief, Dr. Chester and I investigated several convents in and near San Francisco.

My mother came with us. The answer everywhere, sweet but definite, was, We have lost none of our nuns.

Dr. Chester thought perhaps we should try hospitals, but there are too many. We can circulate them, however, with a flyer, and I shall prepare one.

Meanwhile, what I had suspected had happened, and Margaret frequently fell into trance by herself. My mother, when she was present, tried to remember and write down what Margaret said, but her words were generally having to do only with the daily care of a small baby and other domestic matters that might be required of a young mother.

It must be that this remembered life (as Dr. Gupta Lal insists) or this hallucination (as I still prefer to call it) has reached a tranquil period in Margaret's mind. At any rate, she has seemed, despite falling into frequent dream-like states—sometimes talking aloud and sometimes merely humming or singing—easier, quieter, happier. Somewhat significantly, I think, she has ceased her visits to the poor and sick, although she is again very frequently in church. To a good Catholic like my mother, there is nothing at all odd in this, only virtue.

September 22

Dr. Greenberg startled me with a statement that I had to take time to consider, and I have considered it. I am forced to concede that it is true, and that I am indeed in love with the strange girl who calls herself Margaret. I always thought love was a matter of deeply entwined interests and thoughts, communication in the warmest sense, awarding the lover and the loved, joys and satisfactions. I know about infatuations; I have treated them as a form of self-hypnosis, typical of the obsessive personality. What about me? I am struggling to find some communication with Margaret, but I have had markedly poor success. I can't reach her, know about her only what she has revealed of some past life, or some obsessive state of her own devising. I can't find a single point of contact mentally or emotionally with a woman I thought to be seriously ill. And I feel no joy and satisfaction, only a constant preoccupation. But . . . all this aside . . . her gentle, tender face haunts my dreams and my daylight hours. No matter what I am doing, I feel an overwhelming desire to be near her, to protect her, to touch and cherish her. And I don't even know her true name. Worse, I taste copper in my mouth, and feel ill with jealousy whenever she mentions this Marco of her dreams. I even feel hatred of the man who had known her in this life, and had fathered a child on her. I am in love, and it is a bitter humiliation, because it is against all my training, and it seems to be, in every way, hopeless.

30
MARGARET
In Trance

The years were so peaceful and joyous. Our child grew and left rosy babyhood to become a sturdy little boy, my Gianni. *Il mio piccolo amore.* Gemma loved us both, and Marco was with us. He was not my husband, according to the laws of God or man, but according to the laws of my heart, he was wholly my own. And I was his.

71

I do not want to leave those years. I do not want to go forward into the next time. I do not want to! No! No!

I will not!

31

DR. GUPTA LAL

San Francisco

Let her alone. Let her rest. But every few days, we must press her to remember. She must live that time again, fully, or she will not be able to go on. She must plunge forward, through the heartbreak, and perhaps find some solution. She has come back, she has come back into this woman's body, to find the solution. I assure you, Dr. Sullivan, that you will find that I am right, and unless you force her to press forward in that time long ago, she will never go forward into her real time at present.

32

DR. SULLIVAN'S JOURNAL

Dr. Gupta Lal wants to let Margaret regain some tranquillity.

But I love her. I have loved my beautiful lost girl from the first moment, and I want to bring her back from that ancient time into our time, my time, into my arms!

33

MRS. SULLIVAN

Oh, Frank! I'm glad you called, I'm so worried. Margaret is gone. She went out, I thought to church, yesterday, but she hasn't come back. No, I haven't gone looking for her, apart from telephoning Mr. Wade, and the pastor of the church. I thought it best to stay here, in case she comes back tonight. When will you be home? I'll wait for you. Yes, I'll let you know the moment anything happens. Gemma is here, very restless, and wants to go out and look for her, I suppose. She has grown so devoted to her. Like all of us.

34

DR. SULLIVAN'S JOURNAL

It was November, mid-November, before she came back. My Margaret. My Correggio madonna. She was thinner than before, very pale, trembling. I took her temperature, and she had a slight fever. She had returned to the days when she would not speak to us, but she *had* come timidly back to us, to Mother and me. I hold that as comfort, and hope. I will not bother her or ask any questions, or allow anyone near her, until she is stronger.

35
MARGARET

I could not leave you. I tried, but I could not. Later
. . . later, I will tell you . . . I must pray for strength to
tell you . . . Later . . . Doctor. Dr. Frank. Dear Dr.
Frank. Please wait for me.

36
DR. SULLIVAN'S JOURNAL
December 10, 1927

Margaret came back. She lay ill for many days. My
mother looked after her, although she told me Margaret
gave her no trouble at all. She ate obediently what was
brought to her; she kept to bed but got up, herself, to
wash and to take a few steps around the room. Gemma
was by her side, almost constantly. Margaret murmured,
"Gemma remembers too," and said this several times to
my mother, who could make no sense of it.

Then, one Sunday, she got up and dressed, and asked
my mother to go to church with her. There they heard
mass, and prayed. In the afternoon my mother telephoned me to come home as soon as I could arrange;
Margaret wanted to talk with me. Dr. Greenberg, most
kind, gave me a few days off, which I will make up later.

Here follows a transcript of what Margaret told me.
She was not in trance, that is, nobody had eased her into
a trancelike state, but she told me the following story, as
intensely . . . breaking off for tempests of tears at inter-
vals . . . as if she had lived what she recounted only a
few weeks before.

37

MARGARET

I remember all my life, and I told it. Dr. Gupta Lal said I must. And I was glad to live it again, all the wonderful golden days, the joy, my life with Marco, my love, my baby Gianni. Oh, to submerge myself again in those days was heaven, and even seemed to ease the deep pain in my heart. I had tried to cure that pain with good works, to please God. How else?

But I must go the whole way, every step, I know I must, though it breaks my heart. But just as pride is the father of all sin, so courage is the mother of virtue. I must.

We spent four happy years together, Marco and I. Does it sound false when I say we never quarreled? Well, it was true. We were never at variance in any way because we loved each other so much. I wanted what he did; he wanted what I did. I loved and comforted and pleased him; he protected me, and watched over me and my child, and loved me. I thought only old age and death could ever separate us. And in that I was right.

It was an autumn day. The leaves had been falling all week in eddying whirls of gold and crimson. Bare branches began to show, and I was covering all my favorite flowers against the frost. Marco had gone hunting, mounted on his horse Ercole, with only his friend Lucca for company.

I looked up at the sky, and I saw that the blue had somehow turned cold. A wind was rising, and I gathered my skirts around me, and started inside, to get a cloak. Gianni was asleep with Maria. But before I entered, something made me turn and look, and there came Gemma, running fast toward me, out of the forest. She came straight to me, her tongue hanging, her sides heaving. She was almost exhausted, but she tried to tell me something. She heaved herself up, put her paws on my shoulders, and whimpered. Then she dropped down, ran a little way, and came back for me. I knew at once that I must follow her. Marco must have been thrown, must be hurt. I did not even wait to get a cloak. I started after Gemma, who led the way at once into the darkening forest.

It was a long way, and it grew colder. At last we came to a place where almost all the leaves had fallen from some trees. They were heaped at the foot, and they looked recently disturbed. Gemma went there and started to dig with her left paw, looking at me. Cold with terror, I bent to help her. I thrust away the leaves, I found . . .

(Here there was a long spell of bitter sobbing.)

It was Marco, dead. He had been hacked into bits. I knew, too, who had done it. My brother Cesare, for a horrid red C was carved onto Marco's dead forehead. Where was Lucca? Had he been bribed by my father? I supposed it could be possible. Marco's horse? I had no doubt it now graced my father's stable.

Marco's head had been chopped away from his body. I could not leave it. Cradling his dear lost face in my arms, I covered it with a scarf, and stumbled away, and I do not know where I went. I walked all night in the forest, even into the chilling rain of early dawn. At last I began to see what I must do. I made my way to the church in Montepulciano and, in the sacristy, I poured out my story to the priest Padre Basilio. He was kind, but he was stern.

"His body will be found and given burial," he promised me. "Since he was killed by violence, we may assume that he confessed in his last moment, with only God to hear. I will have him buried in holy ground. The young Lord of Montepulciano. Leave, daughter, leave that sad part of his mortal body. But you, my daughter, you have much to confess and to do penance for. I will take you to the nuns, where you may stay until I send for you again."

"But . . . my child . . ." I stammered.

"You had a child of this love. You may go for him and bring him with you. Pray God he is in no danger from the same villains."

At that thought, that my child might be in danger, I ran, panting and stumbling in my haste, back to the palace, to find *il mio piccolo amore*.

My little Gianni came willingly with me; he put his hand in mine, and asked, "But why are you crying, Mammina?" And I could only answer, "Because I have done wrong and God has punished me."

The priest had made me see that I . . . only I . . . had been the cause of Marco's death. I had defied my parents, I had given myself heart and body to a love unsanctified, I had prevented Marco from entering the marriage he had been bound to accept. In my passion, my selfish joy, I had sown all the seeds of my tragedy. Padre Basilio told me so; he insisted. On my knees, I promised, before God, to make penance, for all my sins, and I began there, with the nuns.

While they cared for my little son and taught him his first letters, in obedience to Padre Basilio I scrubbed the floors of the convent and did all the other lowly tasks I had strength for, and I spent long hours in the church, at prayer.

It was desperately hard to bring myself to do what Padre Basilio had said I must. It was with bitter tears that I tried to wrench from my heart the resentment and

hatred I felt for Cesare, but I must do it. I must pardon
that murder in order to purify myself enough, to pray for
the soul of my darling, and bring him up out of purgatory.
At times, even deep in prayer, I would start up, stiff with
hatred and a longing for revenge. But at last, perhaps because of my fasting, which weakens the body but seems
to strengthen the will, I began to make penance for Marco's sake. I was able to bring myself to start to make
amends where I had begun my long abandonment to love.
And so, taking Gianni by the hand and followed by
Gemma, who had never deserted me (and the good nuns
had fed her), we started to walk back to Laviano. I intended to begin by kneeling before my parents, begging
their pardon for having disobeyed them. And I would
offer to stay and work for them, at any task they wanted
to assign me, all the days of my life.

We started early one morning, and my child's hand in
mine was cold, but as we walked, we warmed ourselves.
It was late autumn. The road was clear of the snows that
would fall later, making the way impassable. Gianni
wanted to talk, and sometimes to stop and play with
Gemma, but we plodded on. It was near nightfall when
we came to my father's farm.

Someone had seen us coming, and had carried the news
within. My mother and father came to the door, and
stood there, looking at us.

I fell into the dust at their feet and stammered my
words begging for their pardon. But they looked at me
with faces like stone.

"You are not of our house," my father told me. "You
have made your brother into a criminal and a fugitive. All
the men of Montepulciano pursue him, to take his life.
We are left with no strong son to help us, and we will

starve in our old age. Get out, you and your brat. We never want to set eyes on you again."

And they shut the door in our faces.

Gianni's small hand clasped mine more closely.

"Let us go, let us get away from here, Mammina," he whispered. And so we set out, and we walked the roads in the black dark, Gemma at our side. At first I had no idea where to go, and then I remembered the brothers who followed the way of Francis, Franciscans, they were called, or Friars Minor. If I could reach them, they would not deny care for my little one, and I could begin my life-long penitence.

It was sometime in the next day, fainting with hunger, that we came to Cortona, on our way to Assisi. I found a convent and nuns in Cortona, and I pulled the rope to ring the convent bell with hands that were almost frozen. A woman dressed in a simple habit came to the door and opened it, and she needed only one look to decide that we needed shelter. I fainted but not before I had seen her gather my Gianni into her kind arms, and speak lovingly to him.

When I came to myself, we were in a warm kitchen, and Gianni was eating some hot food from a bowl. I was offered soup, but I could not swallow, and I did not remember anymore. For many days. I was deathly ill. The nuns cared for me, and looked after and loved my child. Gemma had followed us, and the nuns shared their scant food with her.

When I was able to sit up at last, I looked around, and I saw that the nuns' house was very poor. There were walls, but not strong, fitted stones. Cold air whistled between the spaces. The floor was paved with stones, irregular in shape, and they were very cold. My bed was a simple cot, made of wooden laths, and I learned later that the nuns had robbed themselves of blankets in order to warm me. They were holy women who lived by begging charity in the town, and who took in and nursed any sick and ruined woman who came to them.

As I grew stronger, I saw that I could begin my penance there, working with them, and I spoke to the Superiora to offer my help. I told her why, keeping nothing back. I had killed Marco. If it had not been for me, for my love, he would be riding over the fields, joyful and strong. My Marco, my lover!

38
DR. SULLIVAN'S JOURNAL

I was content to leave her remembering, or hallucinating, or whatever it was that happened to her psyche, for the time being. For I had remembered another clue, and with Dr. Chester's help, I thought I might have a bit more success.

I had thought of Margaret's hands . . . muscled, firm, with nails trimmed close. Not the hands of a nurse or a physician. A musician's hands. That small muscle just below the little finger, a look about the tips of the fingers —the remainders of calluses on the left hand—I knew that the musicians' unions had pictures of their members, and there might be many places in San Francisco where she might have worked in years past. Or, she might have taught one of the stringed instruments. It would take time, and again, I had little in the way of facts to offer, but I thought this clue, so long overlooked or forgotten, might lead us somewhere.

I was right. But I did not find the truth for months. It took searching. Dr. Chester, my mother, and a friend of my mother's went to every restaurant and bar that provided music, with a picture of Margaret (she docilely allowed me to take several views). They went to theaters. They looked up booking agencies and groups of teachers. It was a day in March when they heard that a Chinese night club, a rather elegant one with high prices and a wealthy clientele, had formerly had a string orchestra to accompany the acts of the entertainment. They had suspended this for a small group of drum, violin, and flute a couple of years ago, thinking the trio sounded more Oriental. When my mother showed the Chinese proprietor, a Mr. Wu Hong, Margaret's picture, he recognized her at once.

"Oh yes," he told my mother, "that is Rita Bard. Good cellist. But she got married, oh, three, four years ago, and left."

Mr. Hong had no idea of her address or the name of the man she had married.

Then, of course, we rushed back to the old newspaper files again, looking for any mention of Rita Bard. But I suppose her life had been inconspicuous enough, for we never found anything.

I was tying in a few facts, though. She was at ease in Chinatown, ate with chopsticks, enjoyed Chinese food, with no sense of its being strange or exotic. Perhaps the orchestra she had played in had accompanied the Chinese juggling act we had seen which had upset her so much. No doubt it had brought the old life close, and she resisted that.

I went to find the juggler in the hope he might have a crumb of information, but he knew no English, and our talk, with a translator, was stiff and awkward, yielding nothing, until I was almost ready to leave. Then the juggler spoke excitedly, pointing to Margaret's picture again, and I was told that he remembered that a chauffeur called for her every night, after the performance . . . a Chinese chauffeur driving a big car.

Well, it was something. But I could think of no further way to proceed. A letter to the California registry of marriages yielded nothing. Rita Bard appeared nowhere on any list, even back as far as ten years. Could they have married outside the state? Nevada was a possibility. I arranged to have records searched there, but there was no positive news there either.

Finally I decided that I must approach Margaret with her name, her true name, and risk the reaction.

39

MARGARET

My true name is Rita Bard? Oh no. It is a name I used.

(She had answered at once, frankly but sadly. Tears filled her eyes, but she continued steadily.)

No. I was never married. I went away with him, I loved him. But he could not marry me. He was married already. I could not fill his life, but I became an important part of it.

Yes, I will tell you.

But won't you wait? I have known I must remember my life. I have been coming back to it, but with such reluctance. Oh, Dr. Frank, let me wait a little more. Please?

I tried so hard to be another person, to do penance. It is so difficult to come back.

Must I?

Yes.

Then, if you want me to, I will. I will do whatever you want.

40
DR. SULLIVAN'S JOURNAL

So I won.

I brought her back. Margaret, my Correggio madonna.

I was not entirely sure that I wanted to hear what she would tell me. But I must have reality. It is what I advise all my patients. You must accept reality. I had been struggling to find the way to persuade Margaret, my love, to return to reality. And now that she was ready at last, I was reluctant. But I couldn't let her see this.

"Yes, you must return, fully, to this life, to today, to what is real, to the world, " I told her. And she, persuaded by my constant attention—and yes, I am sure of it, by my love, which she felt, if she did not acknowledge—agreed.

And as she spoke, I suddenly realized that the clue word that would have brought her back, months before, had been there all the time, at my hand.

Not love. Not loneliness. Not faith.

The clue word was penitence.

Penance.

PART III

1
MARGARET'S STORY

My name is Margherita Bardini.

I was born in Monterey, California, within the sound of the sea.

My father was a fisherman, son of a fish canner. They were Sicilians, gray-eyed Sicilians, blonds. It was my grandmother, from Northern Italy, who had the black eyes, black hair, and passionate temperament associated with the Latin character. She was born in Cortona, and was named for the saint venerated by that city, Margherita da Cortona. And I was named for her.

While she lived in Cortona, my grandmother, La Nonna, visited her saint every day, and always remained intensely devoted to her. When I was born, and named for her, La Nonna determined that I, too, must be a saint, and she educated me toward that end. I lived with La Nonna because of my mother's illness, and she had great influence over me. I will go back a little to tell about this.

La Nonna's father had brought his young family to the United States, and they made their way west to California. He made a moderate fortune in real estate, and the family lived in Monterey, where there was a growing Italian colony because of the fishing. There La Nonna met and married my grandfather, a Sicilian. He spoke little English, but he had a good business head, and from owning one fishing boat and then two, he went on to start a modest fish-canning business. In those days there were great runs of sardine and salmon in Monterey Bay, and other fishes, too. By the time I was born, my grandfather was a power on the waterfront.

My grandparents had two sons, Angelo, who died at two of diphtheria, and my father, Benvenuto, who was of course called Ben by his American friends. And he had many such friends, having been born and educated there and because, as a young man, he preferred the sea to anything on land, and dedicated himself to taking out fishing parties in the bay and beyond. Il Nonno gave him a boat, and with it, my father earned a pleasant living. Parties used to come from some distance to go out on Ben Bardini's boat. One such party was that of Charles Hebbling, a rich San Franciscan. Mr. Hebbling came down to go out with Father several times a year. And so my father met and fell in love with my mother, Clare Hebbling.

My mother was tall and slim, a silvery blonde. A dreamy and romantic girl, she had decided upon a life in music for herself, and as she was an only child, her parents tried to secure this for her. She had a sweet pure soprano voice, not strong, and not of unusual range. She studied singing and piano, and was asked to sing at parties and at church, but this was not enough for her. She wanted to be an opera star. Accordingly, her doting parents took her to Italy for a year, for further study, and in the hope of securing operatic engagements, but apparently nothing came of this. The blow to her young vanity and her dreams must have been a strong one, but she let it sink beneath the surface, and her parents thought she had "gotten over it." They brought her home to San Francisco, pretty and rich, with a trunk full of clothes from Paris, and confidently awaited the suitors who would appear, the husband who would carry her off.

Young men came to call, and my mother went to balls and parties, but she seemed not to take any of the suitors seriously. And then she fell in love, most unfortunately.

The man was handsome, experienced, and a fortune hunter. A gambler, as well. My grandfather took his measure at once, and forbade Clare to have anything to do with him. This only inflamed her interest, as he might have known, and she began to meet the man secretly, risking her reputation, and her father's wrath. I don't believe she ever actually allowed the man to make love to her, or perhaps he himself was too clever to risk the dangers in this, for Charles Hebbling had not made his fortune in the San Francisco of those days by gentle behavior or gallantry. He had been tough and ruthless. So, when my grandfather found out what was going on he sent word around, and the fortune hunter was accosted on the street, given a good beating which seriously disarranged his features, and started on a hasty trip north. My mother was told of this by her father, who kept her locked in her room for a month, after which she was allowed out again, and her father supposed that she had learned her lesson. But he might have known.

Clare had decided upon revenge, and the instrument of this revenge, meant to shame and hurt my grandfather and pay him back for his rough treatment of her love, was my innocent father. Clare Hebbling had seen the shy love in Ben Bardini's eyes, the way his hand trembled when he steadied her arm as she stepped aboard his boat, the way he seemed always to know when she needed a cushion, or a protection against the sea wind. Clare waited.

In due course, Charles Hebbling arranged for another fishing cruise on Ben Bardini's boat, and Clare went along, with her mother, to Monterey. The cruise was to be of several days, so Clare was not allowed aboard. But she managed, somehow, to send messages to Ben Bardini, who was overcome with amazement and joy. Clare pretended to be ill, so her parents had to stay on in Monterey when the fishing cruise was over, and before ten days had slipped by, she had been secretly married to Ben Bardini.

I can see the scene, when she appeared, after supposedly taking a walk to get some roses in her cheeks, with Ben Bardini, in a new suit, and smiling all over his face.

"We are married," she announced, and quietly savored her revenge.

Poor Father! And poor Mother, I suppose. It was so childish, and mean, and small . . . to plan a marriage that she hoped would shame her parents.

They thought of Ben Bardini as a servant, and they did not like Italians. What of the bridegroom? Was he not ashamed? I am sure he was, and that he learned soon enough what had been done to him. But he loved her, you see. When you love people, you forgive them. He set himself to win her. He took her to his mother, whom he revered and respected, he bought a little house. And I suppose he did win her, for a time, while the euphoria of having terribly disappointed her parents was still on her. For I was born.

All this I heard from La Nonna. My own earliest memories are of a mother already having retired from life. I don't recall ever seeing her dressed. She was always in a wrapper, over a nightgown. I see her as always lying down, on a couch or in her bedroom, with a wet cloth over her eyes. I was taken to see her regularly, because, when she became ill . . . I think it was feigned, at first, and then became real enough . . . my father took me over to my grandmother's house, and there I was brought up.

La Nonna was too wise to criticize my mother. She

called her La Malata, the sick girl, and I was taught to pray for her every day.

La Nonna had not had a daughter, and she projected onto me all her long-suppressed wishes and dreams for one. And, because old people begin to go back to their roots, to "home" and what they came from, she connected me with Margherita of Cortona, and linked me with that long-gone saint. She told me, as I sat at her knee while we watched the evening come down and the lights come up on all the little boats in the bay, about Margherita's big dog that never left her side, that was her protector.

"And what was the dog's name?" I asked, as children do, for everything had to be personalized.

La Nonna was not nonplussed. At once she answered, "Gemma."

We did not speak Italian together, though I understood it. By then La Nonna's husband, my grandfather, was dead, but La Nonna still spoke Italian with my father, mostly to be sure that he spoke a good pure Tuscan Italian, not the slurring Sicilian of so many of his fisherman friends.

But with me, La Nonna spoke a clear, careful English. She was proud of me, and wanted me to do well in school, and also (for she was a truly good person, unable to do anyone a hurt, even without their knowledge) she scorned to say one word to me, even privately, that could not have been overheard by my mother.

My mother was silvery blond and frail; my father dark gold-blond and gray-eyed. I got his gray eyes, but my dark curling hair was like La Nonna's, and as I grew up, it became apparent that I would not be delicate and reedy, but well-muscled and strong.

I suppose I must have been about four when my father

took me to live with La Nonna. My mother had simply abdicated from life and from activity, then. She had been ill, she had had influenza, complicated by pneumonia, and was left thin, anemic, and depressed. I think she simply took refuge in this, and she began to retreat into a world of her own. My father continued to live in the little house, and later, I learned that he cleaned it and cooked, and took my mother breakfast in bed every day. But he never touched her again; there were no more children. And we simply faded out of her life. Though sometimes (I remember this) she used to get up and go out into her garden, and pick the dead leaves off the plants and feebly push the earth up around their roots. When she did this, she sang, and it was a sweet sound.

My mother's parents came and they must have wished to take her away, to have her "cured" or possibly to put her in a hospital. My father resolutely opposed this, and I suppose eventually there was a serious row about his attitude. I do not recall ever seeing those grandparents during my childhood, though they did come into my life later, as I will tell you.

Our life was quiet and orderly. There was a war, but it was far away. We rolled bandages, and we were rationed for sugar and butter. Some people began to use a stuff called margarine; La Nonna despised it. She used oil, or cheese, or nothing. I knew girls whose brothers or fathers had gone to that distant war. But we felt nothing of their fear and anxiety; my father was too old for the draft, by one year. We suffered more, and feared more, and lost more neighbors in the awful influenza epidemic. We were sick, but we survived.

La Nonna was the star of my childhood.

With her I learned to cook, and to embroider, and to wash and iron. She made an art of each of these activities. Her dishes were wonderfully savory, but also economical; she took me with her to the market to learn to shop, and we fiercely chose the best lettuces, the firmest zucchini, the most deeply red tomatoes, rejecting all others with scorn. When she made a cake, she stirred the mixture in a white bowl with a white wooden spoon . . . metal could be tasted, she averred. When we washed clothes, we took our time, and did each piece with the greatest care; the water and the soap were of the right temperature, the soiled places were rubbed out by hand, everything was rinsed and shaken, and finally pegged on a line in the sun. La Nonna's clothes not only smelled clean, they smelled of air and the breeze and sunshine. And when we embroidered (we did several altar cloths), besides making tablecloths and blouses for my mother (who never wore them) and dresses for me, we prayed. And she told me about Margherita da Cortona.

She had been a poor girl, this saint, daughter of hard-working peasants who had vineyards. And she fell in love with a rich young aristocrat from nearby. Her family found them talking together and thought the worst. Why should they not? Rich young men did not marry poor hard-working girls, all brown from the sun and sweaty from working among the grapes. Margherita was punished severely by her family, and rightly so, La Nonna told me. She had not resisted the blandishments of the young man. Indeed, she threw all reason to the winds and went away to live with him. And they were very happy, La Nonna told me.

"Oh, how could they be, when she was doing wrong?" I

93

protested, for I was La Nonna's product, highly instructed in virtue.

But people in love are happy, she told me. They are so deeply happy and wrapped up in themselves that they forget the world and the rules, and that is how the Evil One overcomes them. He makes them bemused with their selfish pleasures, and this is against God's law. Therefore, they are punished, most cruelly.

"Always?" I asked, hoping she would say Not always.

But she answered firmly. "Always. Unless they do penance. Much penance."

"And what happened to Margherita, Nonna?" I always asked, though I knew. It was shivery sad, hearing it again.

"She had a little child, with her lover, and prevented him from marrying honorably and keeping up the family line as his father wished, and she was of course avoided by the decent people, for she was a fallen woman," La Nonna relentlessly told me. "And then one day her dog . . . yes, Gemma . . . came, and told her she must follow. And she did. And she found her lover, murdered, his body cut into pieces and buried under leaves in the forest. Of course, Margherita almost lost her mind, in her rage and sorrow."

"And so . . . ?"

"When she was able to stop weeping and think, she knew she must do penance, and therefore, with her little son by the hand and with Gemma at her side, she went back to her father's house. She left all her jewels and beautiful clothes, and went barefoot over the roads, in rough garments."

"And how old was her little boy?"

"Only three or four."

"And did she make him go barefoot, too?"

La Nonna stopped a moment and her forehead creased, as she thought.

"No," she said at last. "Little children are innocent, they are not to be punished. And they have no penance to make."

This always comforted me. I believed La Nonna absolutely and I knew that her saint was the Great Penitent, and wholly admirable, and yet the idea of the penances frightened me. Margherita would not eat until she was almost fainting, she would not keep herself warm, she punished her body unmercifully. La Nonna thought this was wonderful, proof of sanctity. I tried one time to hurt myself with a little peach tree whip (for Margherita flagellated herself) but I could not go on, and I began to believe, most reluctantly, that I could never be a saint. Though I thought often, as I grew older, about Margherita's love affair, and the ecstatic happiness it had represented, before the awful payment, the penances, the tears, and desperation.

Of course we went to early mass every morning; La Nonna was most faithful in this, and I went with her, eyes still struggling with sleep. She herself had acquired an image of Margherita da Cortona, and it was installed near the door we entered, on the left side of the church. La Nonna prayed there every day, and sometimes she went in the afternoons, too.

I think my mother protested, feebly, in one of her moments of rationality, against so much churchgoing for me, but my father left me entirely in La Nonna's care, and would not interfere.

Perhaps this was the little kernel of hostility that grew up in my mother's mind. Though probably she would have ended hating my father anyhow. I don't know. But as the years went by, she emerged from her retreat into a fantasy world, and began to construct in her mind a net of suspicions and hatreds, and my father and La Nonna were the ones she began to resist and to despise. This culminated in my twelfth year, when my mother insisted that I return from La Nonna's house to live with her. My father, who was fair, gave in, though I spent Sundays with my grandmother always and I never ceased to love her.

For my mother, La Malata, I had a kind of hopeful affection; I wanted to love her. I tried. But surmounting my compassion for her obvious illness was my fear of her sudden exhibitions of hatred toward the two people I adored . . . La Nonna, and my father. I learned, in the way children have, to simply not hear her, to close my ears, when she railed against them.

My father came regularly, bringing money, fresh fish from the catches his clients made, vegetables, and fruit. He was so good, so patient. He had seen La Malata emerge from her dream world into the real world, even though she saw it flawed by her hostilities; he hoped she would one day come out of this, and be again the sweet girl, the pretty young thing, he had married.

Oh, she was still lovely, in a way. She was very thin, and her hair had turned almost pure white, but it fluffed around her small heart-shaped face like an aureole; her hands were fine and white, her complexion was pale, but her skin was pure and fine, stretched tight over her bones.

She almost never cooked. I did that. But she sometimes sang, playing accompaniments on the little upright piano my father had bought, and I owe her a training in music, which later on gave me a living. She insisted that I be given lessons in singing and the piano. I did not do well at this, but I loved the string instruments, and one day my father bought me a cello.

I can see him coming up our little garden walk, among the flowers (which my mother had begun to cultivate again), with the awkward-shaped burden. It was for me, and my delight was endless. I loved it, and I made progress learning to play it. There was a good cellist in Monterey, retired, who had been a player in the San Francisco Symphony. He gave me a sound technique, and taught me, as my four years of high school continued, the repertoire. By the time I graduated, I played well enough to perform a Beethoven Cello and Piano Sonata at our graduation exercises.

In those years, it was 1920, dresses were long. This was fortunate, for the cello is held between the knees. My dress, made every loving stitch by La Nonna, was of fine white lawn, with a ruffle at the hem, and ruffles that began at the elbow and fell back beautifully as I moved my arms. Around my neck hung on a gold chain the golden medal of Margherita of Cortona. La Nonna had sent to Italy for it.

I was so happy that day. Until the evening.

The morning had started with early mass, with La Nonna. I realized, as I glanced at her profile, as she took communion, that she was growing older. Her face had began to fall into wrinkles, and her dark hair was shining with white threads. I felt a premonition of dread.

Then I hurried home to get breakfast for Mother and me. I had bought sweet rolls, and I made the coffee.

Mother was slightly vague but agreeable, and she had promised to attend my graduation exercises, which were to take place at eleven that morning.

It was a beautiful day. The sea glowed like a sapphire, heaving gently; there was only a soft breeze, not enough to lift whitecaps on the waves. The sun shone and brought out all the sweet scents of our garden . . . the amaryllis was in bloom, and many of the roses, including the yellow climbing rose over our porch, and from the beds of pansies, there wafted the most delicate, delicious perfume.

I dressed in my beautiful white dress, and went ahead, to be at the hall with the other graduates. Mother was to come with Father and La Nonna later. I left her bathing; her dress, a pale green silk, lay on the bed, ready. I pressed it for her before going out. I took my cello under my arm, holding it by the handle of the case, and hurried away. As we marched into the hall, I saw, with such joy, that my three sat together . . . La Nonna in her customary black, my father, so broad and sturdy in a new gray suit, my mother so lovely in her green.

I listened with respect to the wise words of our principal, I heard the valedictory, and I played my sonata. I made only one mistake in my nervousness, but I am sure nobody noticed. It was not enough to trip up the accompanist, and I got through it to the end.

Then, oh, such joy! After I was given my diploma, I walked home to La Nonna's house, with my mother and father.

I wonder if adults know how wrenching it is to the heart of a child to know that his parents are estranged. It is a break in the very heart of security, and I had suffered for years, my affections always cleft, not ever given in a solid, steady stream, to both.

La Nonna had made a big Italian dinner, and there were many friends of the family, all Italians. My mother sat among them looking silvery and aloof, but she smiled and she even ate some of the rich food. It was a noisy gathering, there was a lot of wine-drinking, and then one of the guests began to play his accordion, and there was singing. At this, my mother stood up.

"Ben, I wish to say something," I heard her tell my father. When the music stopped and the noise had subsided, she stood up, and in her precise small voice, she said, "I have a gift for my daughter today, for her graduation. I am sending her to San Francisco, to my people, to study music."

I could see that La Nonna, sitting at the table, pouring coffee, was startled and dismayed. But my father looked very happy at this news. He embraced my mother, and then me.

"That will be great for you, *tesoro*," he told me. "You have a gift, you will become a musician. And you will be safe with your mother's family."

I tried to look happy and gratified, but all I felt was fear. I had never been away from my father and La Nonna.

The imminent parting hovered over me like a dark cloud, and I had a lump in my throat that seemed permanent. I had never met my grandparents; San Francisco was unknown to me. I would have to leave all the things I loved.

It was arranged that I was to leave in two weeks' time. As each day went by, I went over all the walks I had known since childhood, and touched everything in farewell.

I went down to the wharves to listen again to the hollow sound of my footsteps on the boards, see the greenish water below. I awaited the arrival of the fishing boats,

99

and heard the shouting of the Sicilian fishermen as they sent up their nets full of the silvery fish, or jumped out on the wharf in their clothes slimy with fish scales and in their long wet boots. Above and beyond the noise of their shouts was the constant barking of the seals out on the breakwater. How I loved the wharf, every inch of it . . . from fish stalls to curio shops, where one could buy shells, picture postcards of the peninsula, scarves and banners printed with scenes of the wharf and the bay and the cypresses.

Oh, and the cypresses, which grew everywhere . . . along the lovely Seventeen-Mile Drive (where my father took me sometimes) with its views of snowy white beaches, pounded by jade-green waves cresting into lace, of a few rich houses nestled back among trees, and of the forest of pines and cypresses, so perfumed, so beautiful in their twisted shapes, as the wind had bent them. There were cypress hedges along the walk I took home from school, and along the way I went to the Public Library, up on the hill, on Franklin Street. I inhaled the spicy scent of them, like incense.

I visited the library once more. I walked down Franklin Street and all along Alvarado, loving every shop, especially the linen shop (presided over by an arrogant old English gentleman), and the Chinese stores, full of silks, fans, jade necklaces, and exquisite china. (So often I had saved up money to buy my mother, or La Nonna, a fine china cup and saucer from one of these shops. Or a package of tea, inside a little lacquer box, each bundle of tea tied with a colored silk thread.)

I walked again along the boardwalk, all the way to Del Monte and back. I took the stage over the hill to Carmel, and trudged happily up and down the streets and into every shop, and ended at Carmel Mission, to hear Rosary (it was sung at five every day) before going back to Monterey and home.

Meanwhile, crying into her washing and spotting her ironing with her tears, La Nonna got my clothes ready. Many white blouses. Skirts of dark wool. Hand-knitted sweaters to keep me warm, for San Francisco was cold and foggy. Rubbers. An umbrella. And a coat. My father bought me a canvas cover to keep rain off the leather case for my cello, and gave me a watch, my first. It was really a graduation present, but of course, it was important for me in a special way . . . my first jewel from my father. It had a sapphire winder I treasured.

I stored away pictures of La Nonna to keep in my memory, and I did this consciously, as though I knew I would never see her again. I took pictures in my mind. La Nonna sitting in the bay window, where the afternoon light fell (the sea in the distance), working on her embroidery. La Nonna in the kitchen, a black sateen apron over her flowered cotton apron over her black dress, drawing up a steaming mass of spaghetti, to try a strand, to see of it was *"al dente."* La Nonna at prayer, in her own bedroom, her face uplifted, eyes closed. And I memorized every line of the dear face. La Nonna in church, her head bowed, in its dark silk head scarf, her hands (beautiful hands but rough and lined with blue veins, from much work) folded in her lap.

And my father. Heavy-lidded gray eyes, but merry. Tousled golden hair because of the curl that was always in it, and briny from the sea fogs. His stocky figure, with the broad shoulders, his walk, leaning somewhat backward, turning out the toes a bit, and yet a sailor's walk, after all, with a roll to it. My father's kind and tender mouth, with the yellow brush of mustache above it.

Oh, I treasured all these pictures, and kept them in my inward vision.

My mother?

I was uncertain about her. She seemed suddenly to have become brisk and businesslike. She invited my father to supper, and they sent me away while they talked, long and seriously. Then, when they called me in so that I could say goodbye to my father, I heard my mother say, "They must take her in and care for her and give her music lessons. I have written them a long letter, which she is to take with her. I apologize for everything; I beg pardon for everything; I abase myself."

"Why apologize?" asked my father, in a pained voice. "Are we so terrible here?"

"You are Italian fishermen," said my mother coldly, "and I don't want my daughter connected with this sort of life, as she grows up in San Francisco. That is my condition. She must change her name. I don't want her to be a Hebbling. No! But not Bardini, either. I have thought it all out. She is to go as Rita Bard. Otherwise, I will tear up the letter and she can stay here and marry a smelly fisherman herself."

Oh, she was cruel. I trembled with hatred of her. For I dearly loved my gentle father.

My father made no answer. He took his cap and left, very quietly, not slamming the door.

I went to my room, and did not answer when my mother called me. She wanted me to cook the supper, I supposed. Let her cook it herself, I thought. She is hateful. Or crazy.

There was no more sound from her, and I was tired and

I wept a long time. I had, in a way, longed to study music, and, in another, scared way, I had looked forward to change, to the city, to the excitements of life there. Now I knew I would not, could not, go, and my tears were of joy and of a mild regret and of fury at my mother.

I took my nightgown and a comb and brush, and left. I went to La Nonna's, and, without a word, she made a bed for me in the room I had used when I was little.

In the morning, before eight o'clock, someone came with the news. The house, Papa's house, my mother's house, was burning. My father ran out, and we followed after, pell-mell, La Nonna and I. My father rushed into the burning house, and brought out my mother. She had fainted from the smoke. Papa carried her to La Nonna's, and she lay in a coma for some hours before she died.

Papa had carried some insurance, so there was an investigation, and he was told that the house had been set on fire. Rags and gasoline were found to have started it in the kitchen. The verdict finally was that my mother had done it, "while of unsound mind."

I breathed again, and settled once more into the life I loved. A life of pleasant tasks with La Nonna, of much prayer and meditation, of happy suppers when Papa got home from the sea, of books and embroidery, and practicing my cello.

About ten days later, they arrived . . . the Hebblings. They had come for me. My mother had posted her letter to them before setting fire to the house, before killing herself.

In San Francisco, in my luxurious room in the big old Hebbling house on Russian Hill, I remembered the scene in La Nonna's little house, down by the sea, not far from the canneries. The Hebblings had thought I would go with them at once, with the greatest pleasure, since they offered a rich life, proper study for a young girl, clothes, travel, all the things money can buy. They supposed that my father would of course instantly agree.

I had resisted silently but intensely; my father had to be persuaded, by many hours of talk. The Hebblings were astounded. Curiously enough, it was La Nonna who came into the parlor on the second day, and said coldly, "Margherita will go. I have decided."

My father looked at her in bewilderment.

"I have prayed. It came to me that she must go with these grandparents and be obedient and good and study. I have two requirements: She comes home to me in the summers. And she never misses morning mass."

At his mother's dictum, my father capitulated. Especially as the Hebblings at once promised to give me up during the summers, and to send me daily to mass, in the car, with their chauffeur.

Only, the Hebblings insisted, it was summer now, and I must come at once, so that we should have time to become acquainted, so that I should learn something of them and of San Francisco, before the classes, which would begin in the fall.

My grandfather was a short man, but heavy and strong. He was quite bald on top, but he had a low fringe of blond hair, and a thick blond mustache. Grandma Hebbling (as she asked me to call her) was a dark round little woman, who believed in good food, quality as affirmed by price tags, and Mr. Hebbling. He was an autocrat, who was certain that all his pronouncements were fair and kindly and the truth.

They were good to me, they were even very affec-

tionate, but they were like people from another planet. I
tried to be good and I was obedient. I kissed good morning and kissed good night. I knew they tried to see their
beloved lost Clare in me. But I lived in a sad dream, and I
was only happy when I was playing my cello.

The lessons gradually became my life. Grandpa and
Grandma Hebbling didn't believe in college. I had no am-
bitions for college, anyhow. They believed in private tu-
tors, and they could pay for them. I was taught French,
elocution (at which I was very poor), the piano, ballroom
dancing, something called only deportment, which
consisted in how to walk, how to sit down, how to bow,
how to conduct a conversation, and other such matters.
And I began lessons with one of the first-desk cellists of
the Symphony.

He was a Dutchman, my cello teacher, a Hollander
named Van Brink. Tall, bowlegged, awkward, with a long
thin face and a jutting aquiline nose and bright blue eyes,
you would not suppose, at first glance, that he could be a
musician. He looked more like a house painter, or perhaps
a streetcar conductor. Something plain and honest and
commonplace. But when he sat down, braced his cello between his legs, and folded himself over it, with the bow in
his hands and the long thin fingers on the instrument, everything changed. He became intense, concentrated, and
inspired, and the most heavenly sounds flowed from
under his bow, as he sat, slightly swaying when he
played.

He was a good teacher, I know. He was severe, and
very quiet. He never let a single mistake, the tiniest
wrong position, pass by unnoticed, but he never scolded.
And when we left the tedious exercises and scales and
played Mozart or Beethoven, his enthusiasm, that of a

105

young boy, carried me forward and made the technical difficulties seem surmountable.

Between classes, when I was not obliged to accompany Grandma and Grandpa Hebbling somewhere (to a concert, or out to dinner, or to a theater . . . and they were conscientious about seeing that I had these cultural entertainments), I spent time in my room, reading, or writing my weekly letters to Papa and to La Nonna.

My room was charming; it had been my mother's, and I was touched to know that the grandparents had never changed it, awaiting her repentance and return. It was large, and caught the morning sun. The furniture was of bird's-eye maple, and the curtains and coverlet were of white organdy. Heavy golden velvet drapes could be drawn across the windows at night, and there was a golden satin puff at the foot of my bed. The carpet was an Aubusson, in tones of cream and gold. I had a small electric fire, for chilly mornings and evenings, and there was a little desk. I kept my cello there in my bedroom, and my music, and when I was most sad and lonely, I stayed upstairs practicing. The grandparents, hearing my cello, thought me safe and busy, so all was well. But often and often, my tears fell on the cello as I worked, and my sighs, so gusty, made me miss my fingering. Ay! Young people can suffer very much, though the older ones don't think so.

So a year went by, and I was seventeen. I lived for my summers with La Nonna, and I even persuaded Papa to let me go with him when he took fishing parties out on the sea; I wanted every minute with him I could manage, and I learned to be reasonably useful on the boat. Dressed then like the fishermen themselves, I wore rubber boots, washable pants, a thick high necked woolen sweater and a woolen cap that I pulled down over my hair. I was strong and broad, but not fat, and I looked just like a Sicilian fisherman in Monterey Bay and gloried in it. The only giveaway was my long braid, so I hacked it off, and my hair curled around my face, just like father's, though his was blond and mine was dark.

But then, before the end of August, La Nonna began to wash and mend my clothes and to pack them up again for my return. On the last day of the month the Hebblings arrived for me, with their chauffeur, and back we went to San Francisco, my lessons, the elderly dinner parties, the concerts and theaters.

I have not mentioned the servants in the Hebbling house. They interested me, from the beginning.

The housemaid was Irish, gaunt and bucktoothed and mean. She was obsequious to my grandmother, and I am certain that she spied on me and reported my doings. I disliked it extremely when she, pretending great piety, accompanied me to morning mass. This began to be customary, and I am sure that she kept her eyes peeled to make sure that I did not speak to anyone, shirk the mass, or take an interest in any of the congregation. Her name was Nora Bailey. I realize now that she was a perfect servant, skilled at her work, and properly loyal to her employers.

The cook was Chinese. He was always called only Wing. He was small, quiet, and deft, a hard-working mysterious little man who seldom spoke. I have no idea of his age but I believe he was much older than he looked. He departed every morning with his basket to do the shopping and he produced delicious meals, of the old-fashioned American type, but he could also cook in Mex-

107

ican fashion (and he sometimes did for luncheon parties) and of course his Chinese cookery was poetry.

I came to love his Chinese dishes, more than any other food I knew, even La Nonna's. He called me Missy Mahglet, and after a few weeks, he began to make little treats for me, which he would leave quietly on a plate beside my dessert, at supper, so that I could take then up to my room with me, for snacking as I studied or practiced. Sometimes it would be a perfect peach or a small bunch of grapes; often it was a couple of cookies, or a slice of his cloud-light angel cake.

The chauffeur was Chinese too. His name was Ho. He was young and sturdy, natty in his uniform. He was always spotless, his boots polished to a high gleam. He spoke excellent English, and once in a while, when driving me to some class, alone, he would talk with me, and tell me about his family. He was married and had three little children, all girls. This grieved him, for he wanted a son. That was the only thing about him which seemed strange, foreign. Otherwise, his talk was of baseball, swimming, and boxing. He never chatted with my grandparents; with them he was impassive, courteous, obedient, quick to act, to open doors, to carry packages.

As many other Caucasians did, I thought of the two Chinese in our household as unemotional, even stolid. I mistook their control, their calm, for apathy. But this was only at first. As weeks went by, I came to know with what a gently humorous eye Wing looked on all the things people did, those amusing creatures. And Ho was fiery, a fighter, passionately interested in causes, as he was in games, and he always took sides.

Grandma Hebbling was sentimental and talkative. She loved to tell me anecdotes of my mother, which sometimes sounded pointless to me. Always they seemed to be about some unknown person, for my mother, as I had known her, was sickly and silent. Only at the end had I guessed the intensity of her emotions. But Grandma Hebbling was also extremely stubborn, and it had irked her that she had to agree to my going daily to mass. She would not deny me this, but she tried in devious ways to influence me against it. It became necessary, more and more often, for Ho to have other duties, and be unable to drive me. And we lived quite a distance from any Catholic church. Also, it often happened that she felt ill early in the morning, and only I could comfort her, bring her hot-water bottle, wrap a shawl around her shoulders . . . though Bailey had done it always in the past.

I said nothing on these days when obstacles were put in my way to attend mass. You might have thought a young girl would welcome them.

Once, when for the third successive day I had been prevented from mass, I fled to the kitchen in tears, and pretended that I had come for another cup of coffee.

"Missy Mah-glet want to go by mass," pronounced Wing. "Ho take you. Latah."

I learned then, later, as promised, that Ho was a Catholic too, and from then on, I was able to get to church, if not to mass, for Ho somehow found himself free for a while, and would take me . . . ostensibly shopping or for a lesson. He had been brought up by Catholic parents, and was still faithful; they had been converted by a Jesuit missionary in China. On occasional rides then, with Ho, I learned points of theology that the Jesuits had taught him, and he preened himself in instructing me. But I was grateful, and neither of us ever said a word about this to Grandma Hebbling.

Managing to get to confession, I poured out my troubles to the priest, who listened kindly and told me that if I honestly tried to keep my promise, and was prevented from doing so, I was pardoned, and I must not grieve, but that I could spiritually attend the mass I held dear. La Nonna and my father and home were in my prayers at mass, and I was utterly miserable when cut off from them.

Grandpa Hebbling had the deep love of music, and of "house music," which seems to dwell in all German hearts. So it was his fault in a way (though I do not blame him of course) for all that happened later, for he brought Einar Flavigny to the house and I fell in love with him.

Grandpa Hebbling was a patron, and a generous one, of the Symphony, and he often invited the players and conductor to his home for dinner, after which there would be music, as the men seemed always ready to group themselves into a quartet or sextet or octet, and play. Grandpa Hebbling, I perceived, was making the way clear for me to play with them sometimes. He was ambitious for me.

The first time this happened, I was numb with fear. I was given the cello part in the "Trout" Quintet of Schubert, and four great men of the orchestra brought out their instruments and set up stands. I got through it, and was even congratulated, in the kind way they had, but such were my nervousness and fright that I cannot remember anything whatever about having played the music. Yet I saw Grandpa Hebbling swell with pride, and I was glad I had been able to please him a little.

Afterward he invited the Symphony men more often. Grandma Hebbling arranged to have splendid suppers ready for them, and music at the Hebblings' became something of a regular winter activity. The players came, at least twice a month, and with increasing familiarity and informality, often bringing along another player or two.

One night they brought along Einar Flavigny, who was first oboe. I had read his name on the programs, and I had seen him from afar, but this was his first visit to the house.

He was very thin, with an upstanding crown of almost white hair. He bowed over my grandmother's hand, and then over mine. When he straightened and looked at me, I saw that under light brows his eyes were as deeply blue as the sea I loved. His face was long, the nose straight and short, the mouth full-lipped. He smiled, and the radiance of it in his eyes was as startling as a cry. Something happened to me; I felt his extraordinary magnetism, but I was not afraid of him. On the contrary, I longed to hear his voice, to talk with him.

They brought out music, and he played. I heard the eerie, piercing tone of the oboe, wonderfully expressive and sweet as he played, and I felt it go through me like electricity. I did not want them to stop playing, ever, but when they did, and polished their violins, and put away their instruments in the plush-lined cases, Einar Flavigny came over to me, and, as Grandma Hebbling was beckoning us in to supper, he took my arm, and led me with him. I felt his touch on my arm like a burn. I did not know what was happening to me, then.

He spoke often to me, and it was a beautiful voice, very deep and resonant, with an enchanting accent. His English was the proper English of Oxford (he had lived some years in England), but his accent was faintly Scandinavian, faintly French. I could hardly take my eyes off his long tanned hands, thin and sinewy—he wore a sapphire ring on the little finger of his left hand—and I could hear nothing but his voice. Grandpa Hebbling had to speak to me twice, to answer some ordinary question, and I had to be prodded back into life, as it were, and out of my dream. Realizing that everyone had noticed my preoccupation with Flavigny, I flushed darkly red, and there was laughter. I wished to die, there in front of everyone, but Flavigny lifted my hand and kissed it.

"So flattering to me, the little one. So sweet," he murmured. More laughter, but this time I could bear it. I felt his kiss all evening.

The supper over, all went home, and I stumbled upstairs to my room, after saying good night to the grandparents, eager to be alone and think back over every moment . . . everything he said . . . to recall his eyes, his smile, his voice, the light touch of his lips on my hand.

Grandpa Hebbling had chucked me under the chin when I said good night, but Grandma looked very severe. I wondered if she was ashamed of me, for I realized that I had behaved myself in a very gauche manner.

The next day was my cello lesson, followed by tea with Grandma Hebbling and a friend of hers at the St. Francis Hotel. Usually I looked forward to these sumptuous teas, for I had a good appetite, but my cello lesson had been a disaster . . . I was distracted and made mistakes. And at the tea, I spilled cream on my blouse, and could not eat the sandwiches and cream puffs. Grandma looked at me thoughtfully, but she said nothing.

I was careful never to mention Einar Flavigny's name; I had a foreboding about it, and feared that they might see at once the intensity of my interest in him. I thought I could not bear it to wait the five evenings before the next Symphony concert. And on the day of the concert I came down with a sore throat. I lay in bed and wept, not because of the misery of the throat (for my dreadful chest colds always started this way) but because I would not be able to look for that crown of silvery hair down on the stage, in the orchestra.

I was sick three weeks, I remember, and during that time, Grandpa did not invite any of the musicians to his house. When at last I was able to get up and totter about, I rushed to the mirror. I saw there such a miserable, sad, pale young face. The dark hair curling around my forehead emphasized my pallor. And of course, I was allowed no rouge. And I was very thin. My skirt hung down, and sat against the sharpness of my hipbones; the open collar of my blouse showed my thin neck. Einar Flavigny must know so many beautiful women of society, I thought, who could invite him to their homes, who wore furs and perfume, who had their hair dressed at expensive salons, and who were worldly and at ease, and lovely to look at. I wept.

Well. It was not likely he would even notice me the next time he came to the house. If he came again. Mostly Grandpa Hebbling invited the string players, still hoping to give me a little confidence, and to see me happily joining in the music.

Dispirited, I got out my calendar and began to count the days until summer, when I could go back to La Nonna and Papa. It was not yet Christmas. So many days! And yet . . . and yet, I wanted to stay in San Francisco, too. I wanted to see Einar Flavigny again.

I became crafty, for I wanted to hear talk about him. I did not dare to say his name, but at the dinner table, I sometimes brought the conversation around to the Symphony, to the music, and to the players.

"They seem all to be foreigners," I suggested.

Grandpa Hebbling looked unhappy. He disliked all foreigners, especially Italians, but he loved the Symphony.

"Yes, mostly," he admitted. "Europeans. But they are teaching Americans. I prophesy," he said (he loved to prophesy), "that in another thirty or forty years, when the European musicians have trained enough Americans, we will have a good American-born symphony in every city of any size."

He went on to other subjects, and I had to hold my tongue. I was to go again for my cello lesson, the first after my illness. I knew I would do badly, and I expected to cry. I did. I emerged into the soft San Francisco fog, and walking toward where Ho would be waiting for me, after doing Grandma's errands—it was always arranged that I wait for him in front of the St. Francis, which was considered a safe place for a young girl—I ran into a man hurrying past. He stopped, looked at me with delight, and exclaimed, "The little Hebbling girl! What luck! Come! We will have tea!"

I didn't hesitate a moment. Ho could wait. Grandma could have fits. I was with him! I went with him into the hotel and into the restaurant, mesmerized.

After we sat, after he had arranged my raincoat on the back of my chair, he murmured again. "The little Hebbling girl."

"But I am not," I said. "My name is Margherita Bardini. My mother was a Hebbling."

"So. Like me, then, you are a mongrel," he commented, smiling. "I had a Danish mother and a French father. Danish melancholy and French joie de vivre war in me.

So you are romantic German and poetic Italian, eh? At war with yourself, too?"

"There's very little poetry in me, I guess," I murmured. "More Italian mysticism, maybe. My grandmother is very religious. She named me for Margherita da Cortona."

"I will give you another name," he said, in a teasing voice. "But I won't tell you now."

He ordered tea and toast and cake. I ate everything in a daze. Afterward, he said, "I will take you home. I was thoughtless. They may be worrying about you." He flagged a taxi, and I sat there with him, enclosed, as we rushed through the streets. He kissed my hand again, as we stopped at my address, and I supposed he would get out and see me to the door, but he didn't. He moved on, inside the cab, and I toiled up the steps, with my cello, to the front door. Grandma opened it.

"Where have you been?" she asked. "Who brought you home?"

At once I knew I must lie.

"One of the Symphony players who comes here," I said easily. "Mr. Agnetti."

"Oh. How did you miss Ho?"

"It was so foggy, Grandma. I could hardly see."

"I will see that he calls at the studio for you from now on."

She was very suspicious of me, and of course she was right. I was ready to embark on a secret adventure, I was full of longing, I was determined to be secretive. Upstairs, in my room, I rushed to the mirror. I wanted to see what he had seen. It was the same pale face, with the dark hair curling around the brow. But I thought there was a radiance within. My eyes seemed to be larger, my mouth more tender.

"I love him," I said to my image in the mirror, and that image smiled back and answered, "I love him, I love him."

The days slipped by, and to my amazement and delight, Einar began waiting for me on the day of my cello lesson, lurking near the St. Francis, or near the building where my teacher had his studio. There was no other way for me to see him than to draw Ho into my confidence. He looked entirely impassive, when I begged him to wait for me a half hour or forty minutes later, so that I could see my friend, but he agreed at once, and even volunteered. "I won't say anything, I know what you mean. You can trust me."

I did trust him, and I am sure he never said a word about those breathless, wonderful meetings, when sometimes Einar bought tea for me, and sometimes we just walked, my hand tucked under his arm, and talked, and sometimes we didn't talk. But my weeks were deadly dull and tortured with longing. All I wanted was to be near him, to see his flashing smile, even, sometimes, to see the droop of Danish melancholy on his lips.

I was in love, and I knew it. He was in love, too, because love is made up, at least half of it, of trust, and what I had done . . . what won him . . . was the completeness, the open innocence, of my trust. Perhaps he hadn't had much experience of innocence before me, he was a sophisticated man, attractive to women. He had had much experience of lovers, and though I learned this much later he was married, as well. But I put all my love, first love, into his hands, and he could not resist it.

But though Ho never spoke, Wing knew all about me. I suppose he had his spies. Much later, I found out that little old Wing, so quiet and efficient in the Hebbling kitchen, was a great gambler and also an astute businessman; he owned about a third of Chinatown. He continued working because he used the money Grandpa paid him for gambling.

So Wing knew about that first time I went to Einar's studio. I was learning about the man I adored at every meeting. He played the oboe because he loved it and because it was a passport to a job any time. There are never many good oboe players. He was also a musician who composed and who was equipped to conduct. He was hoping for conducting jobs, took them here and there when they came up, and was planning on heading a great symphony orchestra as a conductor one day. So far he had not been asked to conduct the San Francisco Symphony, but he was sure that he would be asked, and soon. Children's concerts were coming up, he was sometimes allowed to take over a rehearsal, illness of the conductor or the assistant conductor could be counted on at some time. Meanwhile, his wife waited in France. But I didn't know this until after the first time we made love.

On that day I arrived for my cello lesson, only to learn that it had to be postponed; my teacher had an engagement he could not fail. Something to do with his papers. I was despondent, wondering where I could go to wait for Einar. But as I went slowly along the sidewalk, down the hill, Einar appeared, as usual without a hat, and with his coat open and flying coattails. He stopped short with a joyous exclamation.

"What luck! You are through already?"

I mutely nodded.

He looked at me fixedly for a moment, and then at his watch.

"We have time. We will go to my studio. I will make tea."

He lived nearby (that was why I had seen him so often). His studio was a large room, which seemed equipped mostly with a grand piano and a large desk with a bright overhanging lamp. The desk was littered with music paper, and with leaves scribbled over with writing. In an alcove I saw a few shelves, with dishes and cups, and there was an electric plate. Einar flew to put on a kettle of water. All his movements were light and quick.

I shed my coat and leaned my cello against the wall. There was a couch on one side; I supposed it was his bed, though it was covered with a brown corduroy cloth.

"I will give you your cello lesson, while the kettle boils," he cried, and he sat down at the piano. I might have known it; he was a splendid pianist. His long thin fingers, nervous as butterflies, hovered over the keys, flew across them, touched. They were strong fingers, too, that drew a rich tone and beautiful harmonies from the instrument.

"Let me have the piano part of your sonata . . ." He studied it for a moment. I was working on the Beethoven Sonata in F, No. 1, of Opus 5.

For a few moments, he played it softly, nodding his head in pleasure. "Yes, I know it," he murmured.

He leaped up. "Here. Sit down." He brought a stand, and put my music on it, watched me take my cello out of its cloth case, and brace it between my knees. He sounded the A, and I tuned.

"Together now!" he ordered, and we began.

Was it the specially good acoustics of his studio? Or was it the way his piano playing lifted me, seemed to carry my cello forward, as we moved toward those heavenly resolutions of the music? Or was I simply enclosed in a dream? I only know it was wonderful, a kind of unity with him, a fusing of the voices of the instruments we played, a headlong absorption into the rushing rhythms.

When we finished, he sat on the piano bench looking at me.

"Fire," he said to himself. "You will become a good musician. It is in you. There is passion in you."

I was entranced.

He made tea, and got out a tin box of cookies.

It began to grow dark, but he did not turn on a light. We had sat on the couch with our teacups. Suddenly he took them away, put them on a small table nearby, and drew me into his arms.

"I wish you were mine," he murmured into my hair. "What I could make of you, my little angel! You have so much, all there, ready to be developed, ready to blossom into beauty! The good German grandparents cannot do it. I could do it!"

I had forgotten everything except Einar, and all my protective shyness fell away. "I love you," I said. "Oh, I love you so much!"

He released me, and sat back, looking at me, and said not a word. I was assailed by fear; I would lose him! It was wrong to have told him. I burst into tears.

But then he pulled me close again. He gave a great sigh, and then he tipped my face to his and kissed me on the lips. It was a long, despairing kiss, and then he hid his face in my neck.

"Oh, Mr. Flavigny," I began, tremblingly, but he said, "Einar."

"Einar . . ."

Suddenly he began kissing me roughly, and then he lay

119

on the couch, and pulled me down so that I was lying beside him.

The darkness had deepened outside, but I felt enclosed in a warmth and safety beyond description. I was his, and I felt a solemn joy as his hands knew me and caressed me, and when we were one, I wished that this painful ecstasy would never cease.

But it did. It ebbed away, and then he left me, covering me tenderly with a woolen coverlet. For a moment I saw his body silhouetted against the faint light that entered from the window . . . slim and white.

I suppose I slept. I woke to hear him playing softly, in the dark. I dressed quickly, and then I stood hesitating, wondering whether I should turn on the lamp by his piano. But after a moment, he did, and we looked at each other, as lovers do. The first moment, after the first joining, shows us each the other, as never before seen. He took me into his arms again, very gently, and said, "My little love, my little angel. I suppose I have to take you home. I wish I could keep you here with me."

"I wish I could stay. Forever!"

"I have no right even to kiss you," he said then. "No right at all. I'm married. I'm twice your age. I'm a monster."

I felt pierced with pain and jealousy. He had a wife!

"I love you," I said again, hoping he would say the words too. But he didn't.

He got my coat, he packed my cello into its case, he led me toward the door. "I'll take you home."

Suddenly he was distant and cool. I felt only a momentary fear then. My love possessed me, and I knew that this was only the beginning of my life.

All the way home in the taxi, he did not speak, but he

held my hand closely in his, and he kissed it when we came to my house. Without a word I got out, and ran up the steps, feeling armored against any scoldings by Grandma, against anything. No one was at home, and I was able to get to my room, and lie on my bed and remember and try to compose myself. I knew I must somehow get control over my face, so as to hide the joy of the wondrous thing that had happened to me.

But in the week that followed, I began to fear and despair. For Einar did not appear anymore. I hung about where he usually waited for me. Then I felt a suffocating shame. Was he like the men La Nonna had cautioned me about, who loathed you after they had broken into the fortress of your body? Like Amnon, in the Bible, who loved his sister Tamar until he had violated her, and then afterward, he hated her? Terrified, I hid from where Einar might appear, and refused to go to my cello lesson; I stayed home and pretended to be ill, and in my longing and bewilderment, I did become ill indeed. I remembered that Einar had told me he was married. I writhed with shame and jealousy and longing.

Two weeks went by, and there was no word from him.

I got well, and I asked if I might go shopping. Grandma gave me some money and a list, and seemed genuinely happy to see me better and ready to go out and "get some roses in my cheeks" again. It was another foggy cold day, and I buttoned myself into my warm plain blue coat.

Ho asked, "To the White House for shopping, Miss Margaret?"

"No, Ho," I answered firmly, for I had made up my mind not to live in misery and doubt, but to find out the truth. Was Einar disgusted and bored with me, a gauche and foolish young woman? Or perhaps, just perhaps, had he been ill himself, unable to get in touch, hurt in an accident. Oh, my fancy ran to a thousand hoped-for explanations that would excuse his neglect, that would reassure me of his love.

"I want to go where I always used to meet my friend. I am going to look for him. Will you wait for me?"

"Yes, Miss Margaret," he answered, and his calm tone strengthened my resolve.

I went sturdily up the stairs to Einar's studio. By the time I reached his door, my valor had departed once more, and I stood there trembling and uncertain. I knew he was there. As I stood hesitating, the music stopped suddenly, and almost at once the door opened, and there he was.

He looked thin and distraught, and he stared at me as if I were an apparition.

"I want to know . . ." I began, in a shaken voice, but I was stopped, for he seized me, and held me close, took me rapidly inside, and shut the door behind us.

"Oh, little love," he whispered. "I have missed you."

"I want to know," I began again, but he stopped my mouth with kisses.

"Einar," I cried. "I was so afraid!"

"I was trying not to see you, or bother you," he mumbled against my cheek. "I have no right. I thought it was fairer to let you go."

"But I don't want to go! I want to be with you!"

"I can't let you go, now."

And we were overtaken by a storm of love. I tremble and gasp now, remembering. When at last we lay exhausted, in each other's arms, I thought of the time. It was black night. I sat up, aghast.

"I must go home. Oh, I would rather stay, but I must go. Ho will be gone . . . I don't know what may have happened . . ."

"I will go with you, my darling. We will tell the grandparents."

"But what? What could we tell them?"

"That I want to marry you. That I will write to France, to my wife, to ask that she divorce me."

A wave of happiness engulfed me, I felt such relief, such joy.

But, as we emerged into the chilly evening, there was Ho, in the car, at the door.

He got out, opened the door for me in his courteous way.

"I telephoned Mrs. Hebbling that you had met friends and were going to the movies," he said calmly, and as Einar started to get in, Ho detained him, placing one hand on his chest.

"Better not," said Ho. "My explanation will avoid trouble," he went on. "Better not."

Einar stepped back.

"But I will write to France tonight," Einar assured me, and so I went home.

We rode in silence toward the Hebbling house. Then Ho said, "Miss Margaret, if you intend to keep on visiting this . . . this friend . . . we will have to work out a plan."

"Oh yes, Ho! But how? What?"

"Leave it to me. I will figure out something, and I will tell you both. Leave it to me."

Ho sounded very masterful, very excited. I am sure he was. He loved intrigue, and he loved power.

All I could think of was that somehow Ho would arrange things, and that I would continue to see Einar, continue to be his.

And so I began that double life, half in sunlight, half in shadow. I deceived my grandparents without a qualm. I lived for my afternoon hours, mostly just at dusk, when I could be with Einar. Ho protected us. I do not know, now, how I managed to go through the movements, the empty words, of my ordinary daily life. They were like a dream, and the reality was my love. But sometimes the dreams merged, and now when I think of those days in San Francisco, of the foggy streets, the music and the darkness in Einar's studio, the cello lessons, the teas at the St. Francis, my grandfather's kindly pomposity, Nora Bailey's hateful suspicions, it all blurs into a sort of smeared canvas. Loving as I did, so completely, a love compounded of admiration, sensuality, secrecy and adoration, I knew a fullness of experience that does not come to many.

It was my undoing, my tragedy, but it was at the same time a miraculous gift. From God? I don't know. In those days, I never stopped to wonder, or to care.

Here Margaret's story broke off, for a time.

2

Dr. Greenberg's home was decorated with colored lights threaded among the trees of the garden. Tables were set, in the soft light of the tree lanterns, and illumined further with candles in hurricane glasses. There were twenty guests for supper. A long buffet table, under a row of sweet-smelling cypress trees, displayed a roast of beef over which a waiter hovered with a long sharp carving knife, arrays of cold salads, a hot casserole. A string band, with one trumpet, played gentle music that provided a background for a steady murmur of conversation.

Dr. Sullivan, as was his custom, ate dutifully, scarcely tasting what he put into his mouth. He had eaten thus through medical school, through years of work at the hospital, for so long that the act of feeding was automatic, and meant little to him. Dr. Greenberg, however, seated at the same small table, chided him.

"Sullivan, pay attention. That is lobster thermidor, and damn good. Don't you ever taste anything?"

Dr. Sullivan looked down at his empty plate in surprise.

"It was delicious," he admitted.

"Have some wine. This is real Chilean white wine, as good as any from the Rhineland."

"I never drink."

"You should. It might loosen you up a little. With the world so full of trouble, and especially the kinds of trouble we see and hear about every day, it is wise to find and enjoy the few good things left to us that don't hurt anybody."

"Like wine." Dr. Sullivan took a dutiful sip. It tasted cool, and stung slightly. He sipped again.

"The trouble with you, Frank, is that you are a fanatic, like all your Irish race. A one-hundred-percenter. You are either into something full steam ahead and damn the consequences . . . or you are cold and malignant and watchful. I have known a lot of you Irishers."

Dr. Sullivan smiled and put down his glass.

"I like it all but that word malignant," he commented.

Dr. Greenberg laughed.

"Mind you, I am describing a good doctor. A good psychiatric doctor. And I think a little knowledge of human malignancy stimulates insight, too. But I am leading up to something, as you surmise."

"Yes. Tell me."

"Frank, I like you. But there's trouble at the hospital. I am going to lose one of my best doctors, on your account."

"I can't imagine why."

"I'll tell you. It's Marian. She's leaving us."

"Marian? That's awful! You say I . . . But what? Have I offended her in some way?"

"No. She's in love with you, that's the trouble."

"Good God." Frank Sullivan turned a dark red. He was startled and embarrassed.

"Has been since you came to the hospital. Shall I tell you just what she said? She's leaving at the end of the month, by the way."

"Tell me, if you think I should know."

"She said, 'I fell in love with him and I believe he might have gradually fallen in love with me, but that crazy Italian woman came along and now he is sunk. I know his kind. He will break his heart about her, and she will always be some kind of fallen angel. They are the worst. He will spend his life trying to lift her, wind her up, and get her going again.' That's what she said."

Dr. Sullivan sat silent. The dark blush gradually receded. At last he spoke, slowly, choosing his words carefully.

"I feel certain that I have done my work well, neglected no one. There are even some very hopeful prospects for complete cures. Oh, maybe not complete, but . . . patients who can be released into reality again. I have not fallen down in my work, Dr. Greenberg."

"I know that, Frank. You are more valuable to me than Marian. She can be replaced. All the same . . . it is a rift in our staff relationships. It scares me. It worries me."

"You don't think I should be the one to go? I came to you later than Marian."

"First, the answer is No. You are a good doctor, you are going to be an important doctor. Besides, Marian has already sent in her resignation. She has made up her mind. She has other offers. She will go to another state."

"I can't help but think she is blowing something up into an importance it doesn't really have. I am years younger than she."

"Chronological age makes very little difference in these things, as you ought to know. I will tell you a story. There's my wife over there. She is a good woman, loving . . . even passionate . . . full of energy, still good-looking, devoted, intelligent. I love her, and I am faithful to her. But about seven years ago I almost lost my head over . . . what do you think? . . . a little sixteen-year-old orphan from the Jewish home in San Francisco. I am on the Board over there . . . medical adviser . . . and this kid was having terrible nightmares, they couldn't imagine why. She was thin and pale, nothing like as good-looking as my wife. It was evident she would never be as capable of love, managing a home, motherhood, and coping with life. But I fell in love, like a schoolboy. With Rhea. That was her name. And do you know why? Because she needed me. She needed somebody, and for the moment, I was it. Frank, it's the most seductive thing of all, to a man of compassion . . . weakness. Need."

"What happened?" asked Dr. Sullivan, with quiet curiosity.

"She committed suicide. I didn't get there in time.

Depressive type. Poor nervous inheritance. What you will."

After another short silence, Dr. Sullivan said, "I see what you mean. I will give this a lot of thought."

"Not more than it merits. I am very fond of you, Frank. I want you to have a good life. A real life, full of real things. So . . . watch it."

Mrs. Greenberg, buxom, handsome, breathing forth a strong feminine perfume and pleasure in attending her guests, approached.

"Everything all right, Dr. Sullivan? Did you enjoy your supper?"

"It was delicious. In fact, I may go and get some more."

Mrs. Greenberg laughed with genuine pleasure. "I made the salads myself. Do go fill your plate up again. Let me do yours, darling." She took her husband's plate and bustled happily toward the buffet table, Dr. Sullivan following.

However, a little later Dr. Sullivan said, "But I can't understand it. Me? Why me? I'm such an ordinary guy."

"You are good, that's why," said Dr. Greenberg, his mouth full of salad. "You are genuinely good, and that's still a big attraction for some women. Besides, about love, who knows? The two unsolved mysteries of the ages, do you know what they are?"

"No."

"What did he see in her, and what did she see in him? Nobody has ever figured it out."

"Marian will get over it. She's bound to."

"Are you going to get over what's the matter with you?"

"Probably not. At least, it seems that way, now."

"Well, good luck to you. You said you wanted to leave early. I can fix it with my wife. So, just go out quietly. This party will last for hours more."

"Thanks, thanks for everything."

3

Dr. Sullivan climbed the stairs to his mother's house, his old home, feeling very tired. He was unhappy and embarrassed about Marian Chester, a person he had genuinely liked, much admired. It struck him suddenly that this situation was one that psychiatrists were forever trying to straighten out and get into perspective for their patients . . . Why didn't I, who tried hard and meant well, get any reward? Why did this misery, this unhappiness of love unrequited, or love betrayed, happen to me?

Mrs. Sullivan opened the door as his key turned in the lock. She kissed him, and urged him in.

"It's late," she said, "and you look so pale."

"I am tired. Is Margaret here?"

"No. Come and have a cup of hot tea in the kitchen, and I'll explain."

"Has she disappeared again?" In his weariness, a note of complaint crept into his voice.

"Not really. That is, I know where she is. And she left Gemma, so she'll be back."

Over steaming tea, Mrs. Sullivan said, "She went to Monterey. She left something written for you. She said you had told her to write it all out, and she did as much as she could. She will send you some more, the rest of it, she said, from Monterey. But she doesn't want you to look for her."

Dr. Sullivan passed his hand over his eyes.

"Good. I think I'll go to bed now, Mother. I'll read over what Margaret has written in the morning."

"Will you let me see it . . . after?"

He straightened up.

"I will have to decide that, Mother, after I see what she has written down."

"Your room is ready. Your bed is made. Do you have to-morrow off?"

"Yes. I'm off until Monday."

"Then I'll let you sleep."

Dr. Sullivan slept, in his boyhood bedroom, until ten-thirty the next morning. Then he began to read Margaret's story, slowly and thoughtfully.

Later, he took paper, wrote, "Margaret, I have loved you from the first moment I saw you, and I always will." This he sealed into an envelope, and put the envelope in his jacket pocket.

4

MARIAN CHESTER'S STORY

I was thirty-seven when he appeared at rounds, the new doctor. Short, well-muscled, sandy-haired, with freckles. A typically Irish face, with the typically Irish eyes . . . deep blue, with dark lashes. I was brought up in Boston, my father was a teacher and librarian of an old family; we were Boston aristocrats, the "Brahmins." I never liked the Irish. They were our maids, our chauffeurs, our washwomen. And later, when they became powerful politically, I thought them extravagant, pretentious, easily corrupt. So why did I fall in love with this Dr. Sullivan? He has a slight limp, obvious when he is tired. Did that draw me to him?

Also, he was a Catholic. Not obvious . . . but there was a small chapel in the hospital, and I noticed that he always dropped in there, if he had a few minutes, and I saw that he crossed himself and knelt. That should have given me the red signal of danger. If there is anything that is troublesome, it is falling in love with somebody of a different religion. Who is sincere? Which will yield to the other? And if he or she yields, are they not despised for this disloyalty? Well, after some months, I became so besotted that I even went, secretly, to a priest, and told him my trouble. I must have been crazy. Maybe I am crazy.

I specially chose a priest not Irish. He turned out to be an Italian. We have a large Italian community around the bay. A Father Salamone. He listened to me quietly, and when I stopped talking, already close to tears, he said, "Why don't you take instruction? Then at least you will know what he believes."

"But you don't understand, Father. I am in love . . . but he is not. There's no possibility of marriage. I just want to know how to get rid of this torturing feeling. I have to go on working with him. I don't want to slide into hating him. I'm not a woman scorned. I'm just a woman who isn't seen . . ." And I did burst into tears. I, a doctor. A psychiatrist.

"Maybe I should go into some other work . . ." I mumbled.

"Oh no," he said very calmly and authoritatively. "Probably you were never very much good at this psychiatry. But now you will be. You will understand what gets

131

the matter with people. Now you will be able to help them."

"How do you mean? You think everybody has to suffer?"

"Oh no. Suffering, some pain, comes to everyone, yes. But real suffering is only for the saints."

"What do you mean?"

"I mean, learning to love is very hard and many people go through life, somehow unaffected, somehow never learning. But I think you are learning. What do you want of this man?"

"Why . . . nothing, I guess. I want him to be happy. But I am so undone that it isn't I who can make him happy. Because you see, he has fallen in love with another woman. He doesn't know it, but I do."

"I see."

He was quiet a long while, looking out of the window of his shabby little study. I had chosen a church in a poor part of the city.

"I will tell you how you can be happy, how you can exorcise this fear of losing your control, of your feelings, revealing yourself, and being ashamed, your fear of slipping into hatred and jealousy. Yes, you are a good woman. Ordinary women rush into these destructive habits of mind, and become hostile, jealous, envious. You are not an ordinary woman, I can see that at once."

"What can I do, then, Father?" I asked him, in all humility.

"You must love the woman this man has chosen. Then everything will fall into place, and you will be at peace."

"And if I can't?"

"If you cannot, knowing her near, then go away, and

strive to love her from far away. I assure you, God will help."

"Father, I will do as you say."

"God bless you," he said.

It's odd, but I have begun to feel more at peace already. I will go away. At least for a time. But I know I will never forget my dear, serious, solemn little doctor. I know Frank will never love me, because he is entranced with the idea of saving this Italian girl, who is so strange, so mixed up. It is a creative feeling on his part, I suppose. I would have tried to cure her. He wants to reconstruct her, and in the process make her his.

He is so good, so kind, so *responsible*. And I love that funny anachronism in him . . . being Irish, he is slow, and careful . . . not witty and intuitive, like many of his race. I love his hands . . . long-fingered with oval nails, rather womanish, not like the rest of him, which is blunt and almost heavy.

Perhaps I should rejoice that he too, like me, is learning to love. Father Salamone said it was rare, not many people really do. He is right. I have pondered about this. So Frank is mine, in a way. We are both students of that hard, painful subject.

Later.

I have received an offer from a hospital in Wyoming, and one in Montana.

I'll take one of them.

I have made up my mind.

5

Dr. Sullivan wrote, slowly and carefully, in his journal.

I have been studying your story, Margaret, as you wrote it out for me. I want to see how this eager, loving, wholehearted girl became the confused and suffering woman you were when I found you. What happened? What did he do to you, this man you idolized? I am longing to learn what happened, but also afraid . . . as one is when facing an operation. The surgery will, we trust, cure a pain. But it will hurt, it will require convalescence.

And how did you manage to quiet your conscience about your conduct? This conscience that had been instilled into you, and nurtured and strengthened in the strong Catholic tradition of your grandmother, La Nonna.

The answer to Dr. Sullivan's questions came a few weeks later, by registered mail. Looking at the envelope, he saw, with relief, that it had been postmarked Monterey.

She is safe, he thought. Her family lives there. She is not alone.

He did not open the letter until midnight, when the city settled into silence, and street noises were only occasional and were far away. His mother slept in the next room. It was his regular day off, but he was due at the hospital the next morning. Nevertheless, it was almost three when he finished the continuation which Margaret had written, and it was five o'clock before he could sleep.

6

Margaret wrote:

I can't remember when I began to feel uneasy. I suppose it was the natural result of having found my love, and being his; a kind of contentment pervaded our relationship, broken into less and less often by the storms of passion which had shaken us at first. I knew Einar had written to ask for a divorce, but the answer seemed a long while in coming. And I thought, more and more often, of La Nonna.

Summer was near. I could not bear to be away from Einar, I knew. But home? My father, and La Nonna? Having been stilled too long, my conscience awoke, and I feared. Then, of course, the inevitable happened.

I realized that I was with child. When I knew this, I felt nothing but terror. I had supposed, in my absorbed ecstasy of love, that heaven had been on my side, that all would be well, somehow, someday. But La Nonna's training had instilled in me a horror of this situation . . . of immoral women, of illegitimate children, of the shame. I knew she would be deeply affronted and offended, and would grieve for my lost virginity, my lost morals, my sin. And yet, I knew that, through it all, she would love me. And so, I had to go to her.

I did not tell Einar. Yes, I was afraid, again, to lose him . . . he was so mercurial. He seemed strangely "otherworldly" to me, in his brilliance, his creativity (for I had listened to him composing), and his brusqueness about middle-class morals. He might think that I had prepared a trap, somehow; he might flee it. He hadn't much money. What would he do with a woman and a new baby in his

small apartment? It was not to be thought of. In my innocence and credulity, I supposed I could keep my condition a secret for many months.

Actually, I could hide what had happened, for a while,
and so I did. Pretending that everything was as always, I
sedately packed my trunk, thanked Grandma and
Grandpa for their gifts and their kindness, and prepared
for the journey home to Monterey for the summer.

"How can I bear to be without you?" Einar muttered,
when I told him I was going home.

"I will come back, right away," I promised him. "If you
want me."

"Well, we can keep in touch through the Hebblings,"
he said at last, when, weary with lovemaking, we sat and
ate, and tried to make plans. "Your Nonna and your father
won't want to let you leave right away. I know this, even
if you don't. And I have been offered a chance to conduct
a small chamber orchestra in Canada. I will wire them
that I will take it. I will be away two months. A lonely
two months, my little darling."

My heart sank. The thought of not seeing him, and not
being with him, seemed actually to hurt, I felt such heavi-
ness and pain in my chest. Tears rose into my eyes, but he
kissed them away.

"And after the job in Canada, maybe I should go to
Paris, to hurry up the matter of a divorce," he murmured.

I could not speak, for tears and fear, for longing to tell
him about the coming child, for terror that, if I told him,
all my happiness would disappear like an iridescent soap
bubble.

Somehow I held my tongue.

The day for departure came, and my luggage stood
ready in the hall.

136

Grandma, plump and busy, had bought me a new coat
. . . a soft beige, swinging free from the shoulders. It
would hide me for some months. I embraced and kissed
her, smelling with gratitude the lavender she always used.
Grandpa, redolent as he was of pipe tobacco, hugged me,
and pressed some money into my hand. They were so
good and generous, and kind, but all I wanted was to get
to my Nonna, to weep in her arms, and be comforted. As
I left, with Grandma's last instructions echoing in my
ears, I saw, out of the corner of my eye, Nora Bailey's
dark, sardonic face, and there was an expression of prim
and hateful disgust upon it. Suddenly I realized that she
knew about me. I simply knew it, and I walked down the
stairs to the waiting car, in an icy cloud of apprehension.

Ho was to drive me to Monterey. As he threaded
through the streets toward the highway, he was silent,
but when we gained the open road, he relaxed and began
to talk to me.

He spoke of his family, the athletic events he enjoyed,
and other things, perhaps noticing that my attention wan-
dered. Then he said what I am sure he had determined to
say before we left San Francisco.

"You should have my address, Miss Margaret, should
you ever need me. Here it is." He passed me a little card,
with his name printed on it. John R. Ho. Underneath he
had written his wife's name, Mary Ho, and their address,
and a telephone number.

"And," he said slowly and carefully, making sure I
heard him well, "I can always find Wing."

"Thank you," I murmured, and I put his card away in
my purse.

He began to sing and whistle then, and we rolled along
the road, through the heat and sunlight of Sunnyvale, and

on past, to where I began to feel the soft air, cypress-fragrant, and see the blue of my own bay . . . Monterey.

I could not wait to be home, to see La Nonna and my father again.

We reached the house down near the waterfront. Ho handed out my luggage, thanked Nonna for inviting him to stay for lunch, but said he must be going, shook hands with me, touched his cap, and went away. And I threw myself into La Nonna's arms, and heard myself sobbing.

I can't explain how deep was my feeling that I had come home, where all was safe. Grandpa and Grandma Hebbling faded into nothingness; they were people who had been kind to me, had wished to mold me into something they longed for, who wanted to find their dead daughter in me, who were ambitious for me but who had not loved me. Because love offers the certainty that you are loved for yourself, not for what you may become, or for what you may be a substitute for, or for accomplishments that make them proud . . . love is love only when nothing matters except that you are near, close to a fountain of tenderness. Even when you do not deserve it. I knew this in the first moment, and I went into the house, and into my little room with its narrow bed and white curtains, as if I were entering heaven. If I ever do enter heaven, it will not be with more gratitude.

La Nonna had cooked my favorite meal. My father was there, broad and gentle and good, as he always was. His kiss was the same . . . the brush of his blond mustache, a squeeze of my arms. He smelled, as always, very faintly of tar and of fish. Or was that my imagination?

I planned to go to La Nonna and tell her everything, when we were ready for bed, when she liked to hear my prayers and recite the Rosary with me, when my father read his book and smoked his pipe in the living room.

I had washed and put on robe and nightgown, when she came into my room, still dressed in her everyday black. At once she said, "Tell me, *mia cara*. Something is troubling you. I know."

"Sit down, there in that chair," I whispered, and I threw myself on my knees in front of her, and pressed my face into her bosom.

And I told her, partly in Italian, partly in English. And I finished, "I love him, Nonna. He is part of me, and I am part of him, now."

She looked at me sadly.

"And the *bambino?*"

"Yes. I will have his child. I came to tell you."

"When will you marry?"

"I don't know. He is married already."

Her face did not change expression, but she grew noticeably pale. So I hastened to add, "But he has asked his wife for a divorce. So that we can marry."

"But not with God's blessing," she whispered.

"But . . . but maybe someday . . ."

"You must not wish her, the true wife, dead, my little one. That would be a worse sin. Much worse."

"I know. *Ahi,* Nonna, what shall I do? I cannot live with the Hebblings anymore."

"Nor with him," she said firmly. "You have gone against God's law. You must wait now. Until all can be resolved in God's time. For the legal marriage, at least. You must stay here, in your home."

"Oh, dear Nonna! May I? May I stay here with you? I will hide myself, I will not shame you before the neighbors. I will work for you . . . do everything . . ."

"You will not hide, nor work too hard. We will work together, and walk out together and go to church together.
We will make penance together. I will pray to Margherita
da Cortona, the great penitent. Good night now, *tesoro*.
We will advise the good Hebblings that you will not go
back. We will tell them tomorrow. Now we will pray together. And you must make great penitence. You must
ask for pardon for these sins of the flesh. Otherwise, your
baby must carry your sins."

"Oh no, not my little baby!"

"The sins of the fathers . . ." she murmured. "But sleep
now, tesoro. Pray, and tomorrow we will go to the church
and make vows and do penance together."

"Oh, Nonna. Must I tell Father?"

"Perhaps not yet," she said reluctantly, after some
thought. "I will pray, and ask for guidance." She gave me
a fierce look. "You have sinned and darkened your soul,
and offended God, but I will always protect you, my
dearest child! Always! Always, you have your Nonna!"

She went away, closing the door softly behind her. I
knelt and said the prayers I knew, and my tears fell steadily. I got into bed, and there, with the soft breathing of
the sea in my ears, with the scents and sound of home, I
wept and wept. But at last I slept.

It must have been about seven in the morning, when
my father came in, and shook me awake.

"Get up, wake up," he urged, roughly for him. "La
Nonna. She is sick . . ."

I hurried into a robe and ran after him to La Nonna's
room.

She lay on her bed, where he had lifted her, still
dressed in her black. One side of her face was drawn

down and out of proportion, so pitifully, and one eye stared at the ceiling.

"She cannot speak," said my father. "She has had a stroke. I found her before the prayer bench. She had been praying all night. Stay with her; I am going for the doctor."

But while he was away, as I held La Nonna's flaccid hand in mine, and as I spoke loving words to her, her soul passed out of her. I knew it when it happened. Suddenly she seemed to sigh, and then grow very still and smaller. My Nonna! My Nonna!

The doctor came, with his bag and his stethoscope, and he tried to revive her, but she was gone. He looked up, and he did not need to tell my father. He knew, as I did.

My father burst into harsh sobs, and he knelt and pressed his face into the cloth of her sleeve. I knelt too, and tried to pray, but in my heart were only desolation and fear. I had killed her, with my love, my disobedience and sin.

Here again, Margaret's story broke off.

Dr. Sullivan returned to the hospital, and went about his duties, always awaiting, the thought quiet but persistent in his mind, all day, for the word. It was a month before another sheaf of pages came. Her story continued.

La Nonna was prepared for burial by the people who take care of all the Italian colony, and the priest sang a funeral mass, with the body present. She was buried under a spreading cypress in the big cemetery near the sea, and my father wanted no word on the stone, not even her name, except . . . Mamma.

"Who will know who she was, and leave a rose here for her," he said to me, "when we are gone? But somebody will always pass by and see that she was Mamma . . . and say a prayer."

He would not leave her picture, either, as many of the other families did, and for the same reasons. "Who will remember, and know, when we are gone, Margherita? And the years go by very fast. Very fast."

We went to our silent house. The table groaned under platters of raviolis, cakes, cold meats. My father sat and ate conscientiously.

"I have a party coming on Monday, for a three-week cruise," he said. "I will get ready and stow the gear. Will you be afraid to stay here alone, *figliola?*"

"No, Father. I will not be afraid."

And I wasn't. Not of being alone. But I was so afraid, deathly afraid, of other things.

I began to do the penance La Nonna had told me must be undertaken. I ate no meat, no sugar . . . only a little pasta and vegetables. I took no coffee at breakfast, only water. And I prayed all day, as I went about my household tasks. I had caused her death, I knew it all day long, and at night too.

And I knew that I must go away. My father took the loss of his mother so hard, suffered so deeply. I could not add to his sorrow, learning that I was to have a child, I, not married, not even with prospects of marriage. Where was my Einar? Would I ever see him again? I didn't know. I must go away before my father suspected, before some sharp-eyed neighbor guessed and told him.

So I decided that I must go back to San Francisco, when my summer vacation was over, in three months. The days went by. Father was not often home, but when he was, I cooked, and washed and ironed, and took care of him as best I could; fortunately, I was not delicate, despite my fasts and the hard work. I had no nausea, as other women do, and every day I felt stronger and more vital. People who saw me complimented me, said that I was blooming.

Of course I had advised the Hebblings of La Nonna's death, and they had answered, sending flowers and condolences. Later Grandma Hebbling sent Ho to Monterey with a great basket of groceries and fruit. When Ho delivered them, and we had unloaded everything, including a navy blue sweater of fine wool for me, I spoke to Ho privately.

"Ho . . . have you seen him? My friend?"

"No. I inquired. He is gone. Moved away."

"He'll be back. Will you find out, and let me know?"

"Yeah. Sure, Miss Margaret."

"Give my love to Wing. And here's a letter for the grandparents."

He put the letter in the breast pocket of his jacket, and touched his cap.

But there was never any news from Ho, nor ever any word from Einar. I practiced my cello when I could, but I kept to myself, and I made little clothes for my baby, which I packed away carefully in my suitcase. I tried to do penance and I suffered, but somehow, all I could really do, with my mind, was prepare it for waiting. Waiting for Einar, waiting for the baby, waiting for news from Ho.

When I first felt the little one stirring within me . . . a soft flutter . . . it was time to go. I had lost my Nonna . . . but my mother's mother, Grandma, who had been so kind, surely she would protect me, and help me, I thought. I wrote to her that I would like to come back, and her telephone message came through almost as soon as she had received my letter. She was sending Ho for me on Friday.

This was Thursday, and my father was out with a fishing party. I cleaned the house, left cooked food for him in the icebox, alerted my neighbors (Mrs. Venucci would look in on him, do some washing and cleaning for him), and wrote him a letter which I left propped up on the chest of drawers in his bedroom.

When Ho came, I was ready.

As we drove into the outskirts of San Francisco, the summer faded away like a dream, and I turned my thoughts to the grandparents awaiting me.

They welcomed me warmly, and bustled me upstairs and into my room, my mother's room, where she had lived and dreamed whatever were her dreams of happiness before she undertook to make my father her instrument of revenge against these two kindly folk.

The dinner of welcome was lavish, and when dessert came, Wing himself bore it in proudly and set it before me. An enormous chocolate cake.

"Welcome, Miss Mah-glet," he said, and his old face broke into wrinkles as he smiled.

I cut the pieces and served them with tears running down my cheeks. La Nonna was gone, and it was my fault. I had broken all the laws she had taught me . . . but here were affection and warmth. I was overcome with gratitude.

That night, I asked Grandma to come into my bedroom, and she came, her round little face all ready to be surprised, to receive a present. She loved presents and La Nonna had always sent gifts.

I told her my story, and this time it did not seem so hard. Perhaps approaching maternity had softened all my emotions, as they say it does, for the new life must somehow be protected and nourished and brought to light.

When I finished, Grandma sat, stricken, a look of stupidity on her face.

"But I don't understand," she began. "How . . . when could you . . . oh, he was a snake, that Flavigny! To seduce you, to . . . ruin you . . . and I thought I had taken such good care of you . . . that Ho! . . . Oh, how could it have happened?"

"But," I began, "I know it was wrong of me, Grandma, but . . . but the only bad thing, really, is that he can't marry me. Not yet, anyhow. The rest of it . . . it was like being married . . . to someone you love . . . I never thought of evil, truly. It was so beautiful . . ."

"Beautiful?" she echoed, astounded. "Beautiful? Just like animals. Not beautiful. Horrible, that's what it is. Why do we try to protect our girls? From such ugliness. Nice women can bear this, this pawing around, this stickiness, only when they are married."

"It did not seem awful to me . . ." I murmured.

"But you're Italian," she spat out. "Not like my Clare. She hated it. Always."

The face which had seemed so kind and comforting looked like that of a stranger.

"And I am going to have a child," I finished. I had to tell it all.

"Good heavens! Your grandfather has always held his head up," she said then. "This will kill him."

I thought of La Nonna. It was true. My selfish love was like a disease, to take away the peace, the lives, of other people.

She sat in silence, not offering to put her arms around me. She was considering.

145

"We can keep you in your room, pretend you are sick, with tuberculosis, or something," she decided at last. "And give the child away for adoption. I guess this has happened more than once in the history of the world. We can manage somehow. You'll have to obey me," she said finally. "Absolutely. No more running off, deceiving me . . ."

"I am sorry, Grandma."

"Now that you are caught, yes, maybe now you are sorry," she commented coldly. "The first thing I'll do is fire that Ho. The lying sneak."

"Oh, please don't, Grandma! He only meant . . ."

"He meant to disobey my orders and lie to me. He shall be fired, with no recommendations, either. And you, you *Italian*"—she managed to put venom into this word—"you deceive me once more, just once more, and out you go! Even if you are Clare's daughter!"

She was terribly angry. I knew it, and I felt sorry for her. Like La Nonna, whom I had loved, and killed, I had hurt this woman who had always been good to me, and now, wounded and bewildered, she wanted to hurt me back. But she had said something I must not forget. She had said she would give the baby for adoption. Einar's baby, my baby.

In the middle of the night, carrying only my cello and a suitcase, with baby clothes and a few things for myself, I left the house on the hill, and I never went back.

I had to walk, stumbling along in the darkness, about three blocks before I was able to flag a cruising cab. Not knowing where to go, I told the driver, "The St. Francis," for I knew I could sit in the lobby until morning until I decided what to do.

It was not as easy to sit in the lobby as I had supposed.

Several clerks came to question me, to look at the cello and my suitcase, to wonder about me. I said that I was waiting for my uncle. I suppose they had heard this sort of story before, and were not deceived. But I was not turned out. I sat quietly in a corner, making no trouble, and I was warm and protected, at least. I even dozed fitfully. In the morning, I had made up my mind, I would go to find Mary Ho and ask her to take me in until I could get a job.

The address Ho had given me was not on Grant Avenue, but reasonably near it, in a large apartment house. The Hos had one of the apartments at the back on the first floor.

I was so tired and faint, by morning, that when Mary Ho opened the door to me, I must have looked like a wraith. She gave a little exclamation of surprise and pity, and pulled me straight in. She pushed me down into a chair and disappeared, reappearing almost at once with a steaming cup. "Hot tea," she said. "Better drink it."

I obeyed.

Mary Ho was Chinese, but she wore Western clothes, her hair was cut and curled in the Western way, and her speech was without accent. She was short and plump, and had a round pretty face.

The Hos were Catholics, and their apartment, cluttered with quantities of furniture, was adorned with holy pictures and images. Their three little girls were still asleep, but Mary set up a cot for me in a tiny spare room. I lay down on it and pulled the cover over me, with a heart full of gratitude. Really dead to the world, I did not hear any of the usual morning sounds, the little girls being bathed and dressed, breakfast cooked and eaten in the kitchen. I slept until the afternoon. When I awoke finally, I was hungry, but Mary Ho had known I would be, and had sandwiches ready, and more tea.

"John has told me everything," she said. "Mrs. Hebbling fired him, but he has another job. Mean old woman, Mrs. Hebbling." The little girls, all round-faced, with black straight hair cut in a bob across their childish foreheads, stood staring. The oldest was six, the baby put her finger in her mouth. They stared at me silently.

"Did he tell you that I was turned out because I am expecting a baby?" I asked.

"Yes. Wing knew. He told John. But anyway, John suspected it. We talked about you, often. Mr. Flavigny isn't in the city. John has tried to find him. He is gone." She looked at me with sad, cynical eyes.

"You have been so kind. I hope you will let me stay until I can find a job," I said, between drinking my tea and looking at the small beautiful children. They were softly round with baby fat, but showing the slender fineness of bones that would make them beauties later; all had skins of unblemished creamy white, and velvety black eyes.

"We have talked things over, and we think we have a pretty good plan for you." Despite her lack of accent and her American voice, Mary could not say the "r." On her lips it did not become the liquid "l," but almost soundless instead.

"Wing said he thought you must be in the fifth month by now. Is that right?"

Wing!

She answered my unspoken question.

"Wing knows everything," she said. "He really does. And he will find Mr. Flavigny for us. He is amazing, that man. He knew there would be trouble. He had another job ready for John! But Wing is still there, with the Hebblings. I think Wing knew when you first became pregnant."

"I think I am almost five months and a half," I told her. "I felt life . . . a little movement . . . the other day."

"Well, you couldn't get much of a job, then. And afterward? Taking care of a little baby? Let's be practical."

"Tell me your plan," I asked humbly.

"I am a good dressmaker, Chinese dressmaker, the old-fashioned clothes," she told me. "Rich Chinese ladies pay a lot for these. But I have no time because of my children. My plan is that you take care of my children, live here with us, and I can go back to my dressmaking. You will have your home and your bed and your food, and I can make money again."

"I will be glad to try, Mrs. Ho. If you will teach me how you want the little girls looked after."

"Easily taught," she answered briskly. "Only a few things we want that you have to do. Eat with chopsticks. Speak a little Chinese. Not much. You will speak English with the children, but you have to know a few words."

I settled into that quiet confined life with remarkable ease. In a very short while, Mary Ho had clients again, her living room was the repository of richly beautiful brocades and silks, her sewing machine sang all day long. And she diverted herself by playing records on a phonograph, Chinese music mostly, but some American popular songs, too, like "Who," and "The Sheik of Araby." I, teaching the little girls in the kitchen, or bathing and dressing them, taking them to the Chinese preschool, where they learned Chinese and manners, felt myself fortunate, as indeed I was. I had a roof and a bed and good food. The Hos were kind to me, but not too familiar. Our relationship

149

was courteous and to some degree intimate, but I was subject to Mary Ho's rules and requirements, and I strove to give satisfaction. I washed the little girls' dresses and underwear, and mended their clothes, taught them English, watched over them, settled their childish quarrels.

All the time, I was waiting. Ho tried to find out if any mail had come for me to the Hebbling house, but not even Wing could answer that. Ho liked his new job. Despite poverty and rising unemployment, and clouds of trouble on the horizon (the year was 1923), there were still many rich people who wanted uniformed, courteous, and dependable chauffeurs. Then we learned that the Hebblings had closed their house, and gone to Europe for a year. I would have no way of hearing from Einar; they probably would have all mail forwarded.

So my life became a hidden one, as I waited for my child.

The news that my father had married again, an Italian widow with grown children, eased my heart about him. I wrote him regular letters, full of lies. Oh, Nonna! How I broke all the rules you had taught me . . . every one!

Here Margaret's account broke off, and she had inserted in the package a personal note.

> Dear Dr. Frank. Must I go on? This is so painful
> to me, remembering. Could I come back, and
> tell you the rest, perhaps? Please let me.
>
> Margaret.

She gave no address, but asked that he reply by general delivery, Monterey.

It was Friday afternoon, and the staff doctors of the Seabright Hospital for the Mentally Ill were holding their regular meeting, headed by Dr. Greenberg, chief of staff.

"As you know," he told the assembled doctors, "we have lost two of our most valued colleagues. Dr. Chester has left to take a position in the State Hospital in Montana, and Dr. Abraham Hirsch—who was invaluable in the Violent Ward—has finally had a bellyful, and will open offices for private practice. He intends to go to Seattle, where I presume there are as many nuts as anywhere else." Dr. Greenberg shuffled his papers in an annoyed way. "On Monday, a new doctor will present himself to take over the Violent Ward, a young man straight out of medical school, and I suppose, still brave and hopeful. Dr. Tomlinson, I want you to watch over him, guide him. He'll need a lot of help at first. Dr. Sullivan, I am transferring you to the post vacated by Dr. Chester, assistant in the Women's Ward. I think you are sensitive enough to be specially helpful there. Dr. Phillips will be your immediate superior, but Phillips, I want you to confine yourself in general to records, medication, and organization. Sullivan will handle the psychiatric treatment."

Dr. Phillips interposed a remark.

"I think I should have the authority to assign the patients to Sullivan for exploratory talks."

"Agreed. Is that all right with you, Frank?"

"Perfectly agreeable."

There followed some discussion of difficult cases, and a report on new patients, recently admitted. Over coffee, Dr. Phillips came to sit beside Dr. Sullivan.

"Frank, I'll be glad for your co-operation," he said. "I've been wanting to get out of the couch session for some time. These women are all fouled up over love. Whereas, I see a coming boom in suicides. Read the papers lately?"

"You mean the business failures, the hard times?"

"I sure do. We are going to have a lot of our best potential patients jumping out of fifth-story windows, if we don't get hold of them first."

"You'll never get them first. They are all scrambling so hard to stay where they are, and most of them have no time for doctors. They don't even take time for breakfast. We are lucky to have jobs. Good jobs. Doing what we were trained to do and what we want to do."

"Well, I don't want much more to do with crazy women. That's going to be your province. By the way, what about that girl you found that tries to be a saint?"

"I haven't been in touch lately," answered Sullivan easily. "She went down the coast, is living in Monterey at present."

"You are well rid of her," commented Phillips.

Dr. Greenberg detained Dr. Sullivan after the meeting.

"Come along home with me, Frank, for a drink. I've got to get back later, and you do too, so we'll just grab a sandwich with a highball."

The two men walked along together to Dr. Greenberg's car, Dr. Greenberg with his hasty, somewhat bowlegged stride, Sullivan following, his limp rather more pronounced, for it had been a long day. He had started in the wards at six that morning.

"I want to know more about this Italian girl," said Greenberg. "Reading up on some European reports, I found that this sort of hallucination is not uncommon in

152

Latin countries. Comes from intense religious training in childhood, perhaps."

"It ought to be observed in Ireland then, as well," commented Sullivan.

"That's right. You're Catholic, aren't you?"

"Yes."

"Has it helped you with this girl, this Margaret? I take it you really are keeping in touch with the case. I saw right through your lie to Phillips."

"You ought to be an inquisitor, Dr. Greenberg. You're too clever at reading minds."

"And you are still in love with her?"

"You tell me."

"Yes, then. It's in your character. You are not a fickle fellow, rather obstinately faithful, I'd say."

"You'd say true. Actually, I don't see her at present. But she is writing out the story of her life for me. It is therapy for her, and I have been astounded at how carefully she preserves the chronology of what happened. No digressions, no hallucinatory material. I am beginning to think she isn't a mental case at all, just that she was pushed over the edge by the 'last straw,' so to speak. The poor girl had to live through a series of tragedies, several of which were darkened and made worse for her by the sense of guilt and sin taught her by a grandmother she adored. I feel that when I can get her right up to the present, in her reliving of what happened, I'll be able to pull her back. Save her. I hope so."

"Well, all I can say is, she's lucky to have you on the case. Bulldog Sullivan. You'll pull her back if anybody can."

"And by the way, I would like to ask you a favor," said Frank.

153

They had drawn up in the driveway of Dr. Greenberg's house.

"Sure. Anything."

"I have a sealed letter here, which I want you to date and sign as received, and keep for me until I ask for it again." He took the envelope from his jacket pocket.

Dr. Greenberg laughed.

"You are working out a previous solution to the puzzle, eh? And want to prove it someday? Sure. I'll keep it for you."

Rather solemnly, over their drinks, Dr. Greenberg dated and signed the sealed letter, and put it into a drawer of his desk.

8

When Dr. Sullivan arrived at his mother's home, on his next free day, his mother met him at the door.

"She's here," she said at once. "Very upset. She is terribly distraught. I was able to make her eat a little something. She's waiting for you in the study."

Dr. Sullivan strode to the study door at once. He had not heard from Margaret for several weeks, although he had written to her, suggesting that she return, to continue recounting her experiences, if she preferred.

When he opened the door, she took several steps toward him, and then stood, trembling, her hands pressed against her throat.

"Sit down, Margaret," began the doctor calmly, but she interrupted him.

"I don't want to go on with this. It is too awful. I don't want to go over those years again. Unless . . ."

154

He took her hands, led her to a seat, and made her sit quietly. She was tanned, as if from sun and sea, but very thin, and she was in a state of great agitation.

"Unless what, Margaret?"

She started to speak, then checked herself, and instead stared down at her hands, which clasped and unclasped each other.

"I did as you asked. I wrote out what I could remember. But . . . but why?"

"You know, we understood this. If you relive the old life, in memory, we will find out why you wanted to escape into the past."

"But the past was beautiful, and it had some meaning. It draws me back. Oh, I have to fight to stay in this world, this world where I am so alone and miserable."

"But you aren't alone, Margaret."

"I am! I am! I went back to Monterey, but my father is happy and tranquil now. His wife loves him, she takes good care of him, he doesn't need me. Nobody needs me. I couldn't even get a job. I tried. But times are hard now, and nobody wanted me, for anything."

"You may stay here with Mother, Margaret. You don't have to work yet. Only when you are ready."

"I have to find out one thing. Why have you struggled with me?"

She looked straight at him, the light gray eyes seeming to grow darker, as the pupils widened.

"Was it just to have a . . . a successful case? Or," she whispered, "do you love me, a little?"

"I want to make you well, Margaret."

"But, do you love me? If you love me, even a little, I'll go on with this. Otherwise I won't. There's no reason. No meaning in it."

155

"Margaret, it is a commonplace for patients to fall in love with the doctor. He assumes the place of something strong and comforting, something to hold onto. But it isn't a true love. It is a sort of phase of convalescence."

"I don't mean me. What I feel. What I want to know is, *what am I to you?* A case? Or a person? A person you care for?"

"Margaret . . ."

Dr. Sullivan kept himself calm, his voice soothing. I am a doctor, he told himself, fiercely.

"I see," she answered herself calmly, after a silence. "I understand. I am tired now. We will talk in the morning. Yes?" She rose, as if dismissing him. But the doctor accepted this as natural.

"Yes. We will talk in the morning."

But in the morning Margaret was gone.

The doctor considered, and finally decided that it was best not to make any effort to find her.

He wrote in his diary:

She came back, evidently in crisis. The stay in Monterey had been disappointing. She had hoped, I suppose, to step back somehow into the old life of love and protection. But La Nonna was gone, and her father had made himself a new life, in which he was comfortable, and at ease.

Margaret demanded to know if I love her. Her problem has always been that she cannot live in a life without love, without the total commitment to someone. This is such a rich and wonderful capacity. I see so many people content to go through all their lives with nothing but a shadow of love, if that. Mostly just a series of obvious conveniences, sometimes softened with fantasy. But Margaret is a lover. It cost me something not to take her over at once. But it must not be when she is frightened, desperate. It must be when she is full mistress of herself, somehow, somewhere. Then, then, I will make her mine, my love.

9

Dr. Greenberg sat in his office, facing Dr. Sullivan.

"No, I won't accept your resignation," said Dr. Greenberg. "You may, however, take a leave of absence. How much time do you think you will need?"

"I don't know."

"You plan to hire detectives, something like that? It would hurry things."

"It might be a good idea."

Dr. Greenberg studied the younger man. He looked fined down, thin, rather pale.

"I see that you have made up your mind. You have to have this girl, get her back."

"I have to know where she is, that she is all right."

"You love her, that's obvious."

"I've tried to be patient. I was sure she would get in touch after a little time. But now I can't wait any longer."

"Well, take three months. Six, if you have to. Hell, love is ruining this sanitarium. Chester. Now you. Even Tomlinson might be next. Call me up now and then, let me know how things are working out."

10

January 1928. San Francisco

Dr. Gupta Lal's office was a simple room, adorned with a picture of his guru, Ramakrishna, in an attitude of ecstatic trance. There was a small platform, covered with a dark red rug, upon which Dr. Gupta Lal sat when in meditation. In one corner, with good light from the window, was his desk, and there were a few straight chairs. Against one wall was a bookcase lined with books.

As Dr. Sullivan entered the room, he became aware of a faint smell of spicy incense, like the memory of a jasmine flower.

Dr. Gupta Lal hurried ahead, set out a chair.

"I will send for tea," he said. He went away, returning almost at once.

"I know why you have come," he said then to Dr. Sullivan, "and I have news for you."

The tea arrived and they took the steaming cups in silence. Dr. Gupta Lal peered at Dr. Sullivan over the rim of the cup, with bright, merry eyes.

"The young lady came to me, for refuge, and we took her in. We finished the sessions. She is able now to fall into trance at will, and she recalled all the rest of her life, with ease, and in great detail. Some of my students were invited to the sessions, and I have complete transcripts."

Dr. Sullivan spoke stiffly.

"I am amazed that you did not advise me of this, Dr. Gupta Lal. She was, after all, my patient."

"Do not be angry! Do not be offended," begged the Hindu. "I am merely following the specific instructions of

158

the young lady. She said you were to have the transcripts, only if you came to me, inquiring for her. Only then."

"I wonder why she imposed such a restriction," murmured Dr. Sullivan.

"She had her reasons," replied the other airily.

"And where is she, if I may know?" asked Dr. Sullivan.

"I will tell you later, after you have read the transcripts. She imposed another restriction about that."

At the doctor's grimace of distaste, the Hindu spoke again, softly.

"I agreed with her that it was correct, her feeling. She emerged into this century, with a great heavy load of karma from the past, and the personality of the past called to her and seduced her and drew her back, steadily. She has made a terribly great struggle against returning to that life, to the world of absolute penance of the saint, Margaret of Cortona.

"I believe," concluded Dr. Gupta Lal, with a hint of complacency, "that I have brought her forward. That she will not go back anymore."

"How did you do that?" asked Dr. Sullivan humbly.

"I gave her certain instructions," answered the Hindu. "I am a teacher, you know. She studied here for some weeks. Now she does not live here anymore."

"Where does she live?" persisted Dr. Sullivan.

"In good time, in good time, I will tell you." Dr. Gupta Lal waved his brown hand in a light gesture. "In the meantime, I shall give you the transcripts of her final sessions with me. The healing sessions."

He looked at Dr. Sullivan keenly, watching for his reaction.

"I am grateful to you, and if you have healed her, as you say, I will be grateful all my life."

159

"I did not heal her," replied the other man. "She healed herself. I guided, perhaps. Showed her some truths. She is quite well now. As I know that you are busy, I will get you the transcripts at once. You may keep them, if you wish."

"You don't want them back?"

"I have no use for them, now. They speak of what was accomplished. I am glad of the result."

"Thank you," said Dr. Sullivan again, and he returned to an old expression used much in California, meaning it literally. "I am much obliged to you."

Driving back to his home, he passed a large Catholic church which, he knew, was the chapel of a nearby convent.

"Pray God," said Dr. Sullivan out loud, "that she hasn't gone into a nunnery, after all. I suppose it might have seemed to her to be the final solution for her life, as it was for the saint's."

11

Dr. Sullivan riffled through the clean typed pages of the transcript, calculating the length of time it would take him to read it through at one sitting. He did not wish to be interrupted. It began:

The little girls were adorable, and though they looked alike, they were really different. They were delicate children, rounded, but not fat, and very strong. All had black hair, cut short and with bangs over the forehead, almond-shaped black eyes, small wide noses, little pink mouths like strawberries. The Chinese smell children, sniff them, like scent, instead of kissing them, and I soon learned why. A clean child has a perfume that is sweet and good and fruity. I loved the little girls. The Hos being Catholics, each little one had been baptized Mary, of course. Their names were Mary Pearl, Mary Willow, and Mary Orchid.

Mary Pearl was quiet and thoughtful and obedient; just a glance of reproach was enough to fill her black eyes with tears. Mary Willow was mischievous and willful, but very loving, wanting much cuddling and many caresses. Mary Orchid was still almost a baby, only two. I took care of the little ones at home, feeding them, bathing them, seeing that they had their naps, that they played, and learned some simple things. Sometimes I did shopping for Mrs. Ho. Otherwise I kept to myself. I wrote to my father sometimes, but always without telling him anything. When I could, I put a mute on my cello, and practiced. I had to keep something of my music, and it was a comfort for me. All the while I was waiting to hear from Einar, but there was never any news. Ho was in contact with Wing, and Wing said that Grandma Hebbling had found the letters addressed to me from France, and always tore them up. This was before they closed the house and went to Europe. I had to begin to plan a life without Einar. But I put it off. I was approaching my own time to give birth, and I had never seen a doctor. Mary Ho told me that a Chinese midwife would take care of me, and I would be allowed to stay and take care of my baby, and continue to help her with the little girls.

I suppose I was like a frightened animal in a hole, hiding from danger. So the months went by. In January, I felt the first pains, and Mary Ho took the little girls into her bedroom, to leave the children's room to me for my ordeal. And it was an ordeal, though it could have been worse, I suppose. The midwife said it was a normal birth. But it took me fourteen hours of straining and striving. I had no anesthetic, but Mary Ho and Mrs. Lum made me take much hot tea, various kinds, perhaps there was some pain-killer in them. I don't know. I only know that at last they put a little baby boy into my arms, a baby boy, perfect in every way, but crumpled like a rose. I had milk to feed him, and for a week I lay in a happy daze, resting, holding my baby, giving thanks to God that he was mine.

When I could get up and walk about, we took my baby to the Old St. Mary's Church and had him baptized. I named him for my kind friend, John Ho Bardini. I thought a long time about giving him Einar's name, Flavigny. But then at last, I decided against that. If Einar had forgotten me, he should not know about his child. Besides, on the church register, it was noted that he was "a natural" child, the mother unmarried. But anyway, he received the chrism and the blessing, my little love, and he was under the protection of the church and saints. And I loved him with all my heart.

I longed to take him to Monterey, to show him to my father, but I knew that I must not. The Italian colony was close-knit and pious, and I must not shame Ben Bardini, who was such a respected leader among them, so proud of La Nonna's memory. Keeping my beautiful small son a secret was part of my penance, I supposed, and it was painful.

I went back to my cubicle of a room; there was space for my baby's little bassinet, a box for his clothes and covers, and I bathed him every day in the warm kitchen.

Having my Johnny Ho so close, I could resume helping

Mary Ho, and she began reaping the reward of her industry. More and more orders came in for her, and she was making money. She told me candidly that she and Ho planned to buy automobiles, more and more of them, as they could, for Ho wanted to operate a business of taxis and limousines, and they were saving up every cent for this. It was only three months after my baby was born that Ho gave up his job as chauffeur and bought his first limousine. He began to take daily orders to carry people to the theater, to the opera, or on trips down the Peninsula.

One day Mary Ho told me that she would have to have the little room where I lived with my baby, as her cousin from Hawaii was coming to live with them, and help her, and would use that space.

Before I could voice my consternation, she went on quickly in her brisk and dry way.

"But I have made plans for you, Margaret. Mrs. Chen, on the next floor, has never had children, and she would love to have a baby in her house. I spoke to her, and she will rent you a nice bedroom, and let you keep Johnny Ho there. Rent is low . . . six dollars a week."

"But . . ." I began. She interrupted.

"And you can go to work again, Margaret. You should. It is all arranged. Wing is coming. He will tell you about it."

Indeed Wing arrived, followed by two waiters who brought in a hot steaming supper of many wonderful dishes. Wing, wearing his plain black suit with the high collar, as always, was smiling and merry. He produced presents for each little girl—stretched silk fans with designs painted on them, bracelets in shining goldstone, and a dish of lilies for Mary Ho. I had not realized until I began hearing the rockets and firecrackers that it was Chinese New Year. And there was a gift for me, though it had been gift enough to see Wing's kind wrinkled face again.

"For Missy Mah-glet," he said, holding out a package for me. Inside was a beautiful white silk scarf, embroidered with a design of peonies. I was so touched; he must have remembered that I always laid a scarf across my dress where the top of the cello moved against it.

"For playing music," he explained, reading my mind, and showing me that he had remembered. "For when working," he went on. "For new job. Big work. Plenty pay."

I looked bewildered, and I could see that he enjoyed my confusion. Then he said, "Missy Mah-glet, you come to work in night-club lestaulant. Small piece orchestra. Piano, viorin, dlum, clalinet, and you. Cello. You play cello."

A few questions made it clear. Wing had got me a job playing the cello. I was to report for rehearsal in a week's time. The orchestra would play standard arrangements of known popular semiclassic pieces, to accompany the dancers, jugglers, acrobats and other turns at a Chinese night club. The pay was to be twenty dollars a week. I quickly calculated. My room rent. Food. I would even be able to set aside a dollar or two a week. With so many people out of work, with so much desperate unemployment already showing itself in the city, I would be fortunate indeed.

I stayed home with my baby and Mary Orchid, who was very sleepy after her unaccustomed big supper, while the Hos and Wing and the two older little girls went out to watch the "dragon" cavort in the streets of San Francisco (twenty or thirty Chinese men under the long painted cloth body of the serpent, with its decorated and fantastic head, breathing fire). We were asleep when they all came home. But I asked Mary Ho how Wing, dear old Wing, had managed this job for me.

"Easy," she said, smiling. "He owns the night club."

The first thing I had to do was tune up my cello and practice. I had lost my calluses, but they came back, painfully enough. And my little Johnny Ho seemed to enjoy listening to me work. His eyes had opened, big blue eyes like his father's, and he turned his head toward the sound I made.

On the first of the month, I moved into Mrs. Chen's back bedroom, and I saw that she, trembling with pleasure as I let her hold Johnny Ho, had even provided a baby bed for him, with a draped mosquito net. She was a round, shapeless Chinese lady of the old school, who spoke almost no English (but I had enough Chinese by then to manage the few words we needed). She was always dressed in a black satin coat and trousers, and wore velvet flat slippers on her small feet. Her hair was combed simply back from a round forehead and fastened into a bun at the back of her neck. She was a widow, childless, a very unhappy situation in Chinatown. She had many relatives who came in to see her, and to sit and chatter and eat lichee nuts, scattering the brown crisp shells on the floor, and many of them wanted to hold Johnny Ho. I worried about this, but as I did not have to go out to rehearsal until about five in the afternoons, I came to rely on Mrs. Chen to watch over my baby for me when I was gone. She seemed to live for this, and to await the moment when I put him, fed and bathed and already sleepy, into her arms, just before I left with my cello.

Mary Ho's cousin Ruby had arrived—such a little girl, only fourteen, I thought, but I learned later that she was twenty—and I sometimes went in to help out when I could, during the day, when I was quite free.

Mary Ho made me a dress for my work in the orchestra at the night club. It was a slim sheath of soft pink brocade, with a high fitted collar, slit up each side to mid-thigh, but I wore a pleated underskirt of pale pink georgette. It was unexpectedly comfortable for playing the cello.

The "orchestra," so called, was a scratch affair. The pianist was a lady more than middle-aged, perhaps verging on sixty, but she had dyed her hair, and was slim and sprightly, as well as very competent. We all followed her, though properly the violinist should have been the leader. But Mrs. Harmon, the pianist, had been accompanying vaudeville acts for so long that she knew every change of rhythm, every instant when musicians should be silent and let the drummer roll up an increasing drumbeat to rivet the attention of the public on the performer. The violinist was her daughter, Eileen, who played carefully, and was dependable. The clarinetist, I soon saw, was Eileen's boy friend. He was not very good, and Mrs. Harmon made many cuts in his music, letting him manage the occasional melodic solos, or slow waltzes, for the jugglers. There were always Chinese jugglers at the night club, and I never ceased to marvel at their skill. I found out that they had trained since childhood, and still practiced hours every day. I was given melodic sections to play—especially the ones the clarinet couldn't manage—and I soon picked up the peculiar style of an accompanying ensemble. The drummer was our star, and he was Chinese, a bright-eyed boy who adored his drums and triangles and cymbals, and the rest of the noisemakers of his trade. He had superb rhythm, and he never seemed to tire of working in variations in his drumbeats. His name was Sidney Kee.

After my initial nervousness, I fell in with the requirements of my job, and even began to enjoy it. For one thing, besides my pay, I was given a good supper every night, at the orchestra break before the second show, and Ho called for me every night when work was over, and drove me home in his limousine. This aroused much comment, and I was sometimes addressed as "Your Highness," but only in good-natured teasing. I had learned that the Chinese love to tease, and that their bright eyes never missed any sign of pomposity or pretense. Ho, I think, really enjoyed showing off his splendid big car, but also, he was protective of me, for had I not named my son for him? He loved little Johnny Ho, and I knew he longed for a son of his own. He and Mary were awaiting another child, while she cut and basted and made her sewing machine hum, and of course, this time, they hoped for a boy.

I gave my name as Rita Bard, as my mother had instructed, years before. It was not in deference to her memory—I thought of her in an uneasy way, for I had both loved and resented her—but simply because it was the easiest thing to do. If I had used the name Hebbling, or even Bardini, it might have saved me time and tearful nights, for when Einar came to San Francisco to look for me, the Chinese said only Miss Bard (which sounded, in their mouths, like Bod, or Bond) worked as a cellist in the club.

I had no idea that Einar was searching for me. I had

given him up, as a sort of dream, and I never looked ahead for more than a day. The only thing I did was keep up a sort of correspondence with my father. It is amazing, how often one can write to a loved person and say little or nothing. News, as such, can be so trivial and one can hide behind affectionate phrases that tell little of the truth.

And so my life was uneventful, even hidden still. I seldom saw anyone other than my Chinese friends. I helped Mary Ho and Mrs. Chen, I tended my baby; in the evenings I went to work with my cello, and played the simple tunes that were required. Time passed.

Mary Ho had her baby. Another girl. She was very angry about this for a while, but her natural goodness and her Christian faith sustained her, and after about a week she began to love and cuddle the new black-haired doll as she had the others. The cousin, Ruby, took over the care of the tiny one, and Mary Ho went back to her sewing machine. The new baby was named Mary Margaret, for me, but soon everyone called her Mei Mei, which means Little Sister in Chinese. And we all loved her.

This was my life.

Until an evening in October. It had been one of those heavenly blue evenings, when the color in the sky seems to wash down over the buildings and hang in the windows, turning them to sheets of sapphire until the stars come out. We had a good show at the club, one lasting about fifteen minutes longer than the previous one. There were two Chinese jugglers who lay on their backs on inclined couches and kept barrels spinning with their feet. Then these barrels were passed from one to the other, in a display of skill that was really astounding. After the barrels were spinning back and forth so fast one could scarcely watch when they passed each other in air, a pretty young Chinese girl, dressed in tights that were spangled with sequins, came out to dance and bob and swing between those rushing spinning dangerous barrels as they flew across the stage. There were also acrobats, in white tights, who performed feats of skill and strength, and as the final number, a Chinese girl, perhaps sixteen, who rode about on the tiny stage on a one-wheeled bicycle, doing handstands, headstands, and various other acrobatic feats, as the one wheel kept up a steady circling.

I knew the music, and could watch. I never ceased to be amazed at the skill of the performers, and I admired their physical appearance. All were small, delicately made, but firm and round and smooth.

After the second show, I packed up my cello, said good night to Mrs. Harmon and the others and Sidney Kee, and started for the door. Ho was usually waiting just outside, in the big black car. But this time there was someone in the car, and as I opened the door, and took a step inside I was gathered into a remembered embrace.

It was Einar. He had found me at last.

At the moment I felt Einar's arms around me, I knew what I had been waiting for, longing, for, even though this fierce hunger had lain deep inside me, unacknowledged for so many months.

Ho silently took us to a hotel, and Einar led me in, like a somnambulist. I knew that Mrs. Chen would care for my baby. I could not speak or ask any questions for a long time, nor could Einar. In each other's arms, we tried to make up for the lost months, for the longing, the fears. However, with morning light we had to talk, and I told him that I had chosen to leave my grandparents' house and hide. I told him about Johnny Ho. I told him about

La Nonna, and how my condition and my apparent abandonment had caused her death. He did not protest, he
only held me close, and I knew that he understood everything. In fragments, I learned about what his life had
been.

He had written to me, at the Hebblings', but had no
answer. Trying to think that I was very young, and that I
had probably found other friends, he stopped writing
then. But later, in Paris, he had dreamed of me, and knew
that he loved me. He had asked his wife, again, for a divorce, but had been given only denial and scorn. Then he
tried to write to me, care of my old cello teacher, but his
letter had been returned. Afterward, though he knew the
United States was experiencing a depression and that jobs
were few, he heard that some private colleges were hiring
composers to teach music, to give a certain éclat to their
courses. So Einar had pulled strings and used what
friends in Europe he had who could help, and he had se-
cured a place as resident composer-teacher at a small college in California, north of San Francisco. Every weekend
he had free he had come to San Francisco to look for me.
For weeks he had hung about near where we used to
meet, he had sat in the lobby of the St. Francis, he had
walked the streets, looking, looking. Then one day, he
saw Ho, driving his limousine. He ran after Ho for three
blocks, and at last Ho stopped, and they recognized each
other. And so he had learned about me, about the job at
the night club, and about my . . . our . . . Johnny Ho.

"My little love, to go through all this alone," he grieved,
his cheek pressed to mine.

"But I wasn't alone," I answered. "The Hos were so
good to me. And Wing, and Mrs. Chen."

"But now you will come and be with me."

I simply accepted that, without thinking anymore. After we dressed and had breakfast, we went to my house to meet Mrs. Chen, and Einar held his son in his arms, at last.

"I never thought to have a son," he whispered. And he said all the old words, repeated so often, by so many. "It is wonderful. He is beautiful, our son." I was deeply content. Only Mrs. Chen was sad, for she knew at once that we would be going away.

I left all plans to Einar, but in the end it turned out that he could not take us to live with him at the college. He had rooms in a dormitory, and in his contract had not said that he had a wife and son. He had to return to his work and the college, but I stayed on at Mrs. Chen's, in a daze of happiness. He came to us every weekend. But the third weekend he had a plan. Through a colleague at the college where he was teaching, Einar heard of a cottage that would be free for rent, on the Big Sur road south of Monterey. He had bought a secondhand car, and we ventured down the Peninsula to Monterey and beyond to find it. It was just what we wanted, a studio-cottage, standing high over the rocks, with the sea washing in below at high tide. The young painter-owner was going to Europe for a year, and would rent it cheap. Einar inspected the foundations, found them safe, and liked the studio. There was a slanted roof, partly glass, for the north light, but a good fireplace, for warmth. It was only one room, but it was spacious enough. There was a tiny bath, and to one side of the studio was a small electric stove, with a few essential pots and pans, coffeepot, plates, and cups. Couches were both beds and chairs. There was a rough table. No carpets or curtains. The windows were toward the sea, and the place was decorated only with a few hanging nets and Japanese glass floats in shimmering colors.

"It's lacking two things only," Einar told the artist. "A cradle, and a music stand. My wife is a cellist."

There it was. We were not married, and probably never would be. But he was introducing me as his wife.

"I've a pal down the way who works in wood; name's Paul Gage," said the artist, pocketing the first month's rent and signing a letter of agreement with Einar. "He can probably knock up a few bits of furniture for you, if you need them.

"He's a nice guy. You can arrange for him to bring you some bread and milk and supplies when he goes to town once a week, if you like. Paul does this for several of the neighbors. We have a sort of little community, here. Cookouts sometimes. Sing songs. We don't live in each other's pockets but we look out for each other. Oh, and there's a doctor down the way. Sorry I have no phone, but a friend about half a mile down the road has one, and he will lend it any time, or take messages. He has a motorbike, and gets over right away if you need to know something in a hurry."

We met that young man, whose name was Wesley Hand, later, and he was kindness itself, often riding up in a great roar and a dust cloud, to ask if he could do any errands for me in Monterey.

But first, we had the sad duty of saying goodbye to Mrs. Chen and Wing and the Hos. I invited them all to come and see us, though I knew in my heart they never would. Chinese people are not great visitors. And I promised to come back often to them, and I did manage it once or twice.

I had few enough possessions, and when Einar came,

on the weekends, he brought a suitcase with his own things. What were mine? My cello, some music, my baby, and his little sweaters and coats and diapers, and the beautiful dress Mary Ho had made for me, but clothes were not important for me. Life was informal; I lived in dark skirts and blouses, a smock or two.

Then began another kind of life for me, again, a hidden, quiet life but sustained by love. It was all I wanted, all I needed, and I often stopped to wonder at my good fortune. How many people in the world, I mused, had everything they wanted, all at once, in full measure, as I did? I had my lover, my child, my safe home, warmth and food, and the glorious sea before my eyes, every day and every night. And how I loved the sea! In the mornings, it was silken, shining silver gray, smooth as pearl. By noon it was a deep sapphire blue, often with whitecaps riding the crests of the waves the wind tossed. At sunset it glowed with rose and purple and gold. And at night, when my baby was asleep and I sat by the window, I could hear the sea breathing, like a living thing, and I was never lonely.

When Einar came, it was heaven, and all the week, between his visits, was a time of joyful waiting and preparation. I cooked good meals and served them carefully. I kept my baby and my house clean.

Not long after I had moved into the cottage, Einar managed to rent an old upright piano, which came by truck, and was somehow manipulated into the studio, two men carrying it up the sandy path between the rocks and the clumps of pink sand flowers that grew around them. Then our weekends were full of music, and I had more direction for my practicing. And, using our table—where we ate, where I sewed, where we sat and talked over coffee—

Einar spread out his music paper and composed. One of his songs became very popular, "Lullaby for a Crying Child," and he began to sketch a concerto for cello and string orchestra. And we moved in a kind of light; I always felt darkness enclose me when he left, on Sunday afternoons, even though the sun may have been shining in glory.

I was not far from Monterey, and sometimes I could get a ride into town with some acquaintance who was going that way. And so, about three months after we were established at "Rock Cottage," I dressed my baby—by now almost seven months old—and went to find my father.

Mr. Hand got us a ride with a friend who was going to Carmel, and from there we took the bus that now went four times a day up over the hill, and then down into the town. Johnny Ho was good, interested in everything and everyone, getting very heavy for me to hold. Besides I had to carry a bag of changes for him, his bottle, and a toy to divert him if he became restless. From Monterey I got a cab to take me over to where my father and La Nonna had lived, where I had lived my happy childhood.

To my dismay, when I got there, I saw that the house was deserted, and I went around to the neighbors, inquiring. A few of them remembered me, admired my baby, and told me what they knew. My father and his wife had gone to Italy, to look up the wife's people, and they expected to be gone a year. The house was for sale, as they intended to move into an apartment on their return.

I had known nothing of these plans. It was my own fault. In my selfish happiness, with Einar again, I had not written to my father. If he had written to me, the Hos might still have the letter. I had a sinking heart, as I looked at the house that had held my Nonna, where we had cooked so many big family dinners, where there had been much love and talk and noise, good food and strong virtue. I turned around and made my way back the way I had come. By then Johnny Ho was restless and tired, and so was I. He cried all the way from Monterey to Carmel, where I was to meet the friends who would take us home again, and by the time I saw my little Rock Cottage once more, I was crying too. We mingled our tears over bread and milk, and wept in our beds, Johnny Ho in his, and I in mine, from disappointment and exhaustion. It was a Wednesday, and I thought I would never live until Saturday again, when Einar would come.

By Saturday I was calm, and I said nothing about my father's absence to Einar. And so our life went on, quiet, poor, and utterly happy.

Little Johnny Ho took his first step into his father's arms. But his first word was for me. Not Mama. It was Lob . . . I suppose because he heard Einar call me "Love," as he always did.

The painter-owner stayed on in Europe, and we stayed on at Rock Cottage.

How can I tell about those days, which lengthened into two years with Einar, weekends and vacations? Everything seemed perfect to me. I wanted nothing more. When the afternoon wind rose, and the sea was speckled with whitecaps, I loved the hour. When it rained, and everything was gray and damp, smelling of brine from the sea and wet pines and cypresses and ferns, I loved the rain. When it was cold at night, we made a fire in the fireplace, and sat before it on the floor, seeing each other only in the light from the flames, and often not seeing each other at all, for I would sit enclosed in Einar's arms, my head tucked into his shoulder.

He worked hard for many hours on those weekends, too, and Boosey & Hawkes, the music publishers, had accepted a set of his short pieces. He wrote many letters, trying to arrange to conduct these himself. One evening— it was a calm, cold evening, with moonlight on the sea— he told me that he thought he should accept a few guest conductor jobs as they came up.

"Have there been some offers?" I asked at once.

Yes, he told me, somewhat sheepishly. There had been a few. But they would have meant considerable travel, being away from me and Johnny Ho. He had not accepted any.

"But," he added at once, seeing my distress, for I did not want to be a burden or an obstacle to him, or to his work, "but now I have been offered a pair of concerts in Arizona, not so far, and another pair in Spokane, also fairly near. I would have to miss only one weekend with you each time. I couldn't bear it to be separated for more than one weekend."

"But of course you must accept these engagements!"

I said nothing about going with him. At the college, perhaps a few of Einar's friends knew about me, but I was not his wife; I could not stand beside him and gloat over his success. I had to remain where I was, hidden. But it was enough for me. I did not think forward into time, into a possible marriage someday and life everywhere at his side. It might come, but I kept my mind away from everything except my present happiness. My son flourished, I loved and was loved, and we lived in comfort.

I stored up images, like bright photographs in my

mind, and kept them to think over when Einar was away. The sunlight shining through his crest of silvery blond hair as he worked, in shirt-sleeves, at our table. Einar at the piano, often in dressing gown, with our Johnny Ho, also in small dressing gown, plucking at his sleeve. Einar at the wheel of his old car, singing and shouting into the wind, as we drove down the coast to a beach where we often picnicked, letting Johnny Ho run about on the sand stark naked. He got so brown, and his short fat legs twinkled as he ran away from the waves that curled around his ankles. And when a wave caught him in its lace, and tumbled him, he would call for me, "Lob! Lob!" Suppertime, at our table, with Einar relaxing over his coffee, and Johnny Ho already nodding with sleep over his cereal, but fighting it, and even trying to hold his eyes open with his little hands. Oh, so many pictures I kept in my mind, in a sort of file, for my idle moments. They only hurt me now, to remember and look.

I had been having occasional twinges of pain in my side. I dismissed it as indigestion, and even, yes, I dared to hope . . . even, I thought, it might mean that I was pregnant again. But one morning I woke with such agony in my side that I was doubled over, and my face was gray. It frightened Einar. It was a Saturday, I remember, and Einar had arrived only an hour or so before I was taken with such pain that I couldn't move.

"Love, what is wrong? Tell me," he begged.

"My stomach," I gasped, for the pain was focused in front and to the right of my navel.

He touched me, ever so tenderly, but I shrank away.

"I think I have to get you to a doctor. Immediately," he said.

He brought my coat, bundled up Johnny Ho, and

somehow I managed to stagger out to the car with Einar's arm supporting me.

It was a dark day, with heavy clouds massing over the sea, and as we drove in toward Carmel and then down the hill toward Monterey, I was conscious of the first gusts of rain.

"A storm. We are going to have a big storm from the Pacific," Einar said. "The birds are flying inland."

I could answer nothing. I sat silent, enclosed in an envelope of pain, and every movement caused me exquisite torture.

On his drives through Monterey, Einar had noticed a sign indicating a doctor and a clinic, and he made for that address. We skidded once on the hill, for our tires were old and slick, and the rain began coming down heavily. Once in front of the clinic, Einar left me in the car and ran up the path and up the steps. He rang furiously at the door, which after a time opened. He spoke quickly, gesturing toward me, and in a short while a man in a white coat, and a woman also in white, came rushing out, carrying a stretcher. I was by then almost unconscious, but I vaguely recall being on an examination table, and hearing Einar's anguished questions.

"It's appendicitis, and very severe," I heard. "We must operate at once."

I don't remember anymore, and I was told later that I had been operated on, the surgeon finding that the appendix had burst. I was in fever and dreadfully ill for many days, as they fought off peritonitis.

When at last my youth and general good health had triumphed over the infection, and proper drainage had been set up in my side, I began to be aware of my surroundings, and to ask questions.

Then one morning I awoke cool, and feeling very weak, but rested.

Standing by my bed was Mr. Hand.

Instantly I knew that something awful had happened. I read it in his face.

I struggled to sit up.

"Einar? My baby?" I cried.

"Try to be calm, Margaret," said Mr. Hand. "Try to be brave."

"Oh what happened? Tell me! Tell me!" I tried to seize him by the jacket, to shake him, to make him tell me.

But he eluded me, and left the room.

The doctor, a kind, tired man in his fifties, came in, drew up a chair, and took my hand in his.

"Tell me, tell me," I was sobbing.

"There was a great storm, Mrs. Flavigny. Two fishing boats were lost and one was smashed up against the rocks. And there was an accident on the Carmel Hill."

Through a fog of terror I finally got the facts straight.

Two automobiles had gone into a skid on the Carmel Hill and collided. In the heavier car, the passengers were shaken and bruised. In the other car, the driver and a child with him were thrown out and instantly killed.

They were my Einar and my baby.

12

I have no idea what happened during the next days. Mr. Hand, it seemed, had identified Einar and Johnny Ho, had seen to the funerals. He sold my cello and got almost enough money to take care of everything. The college where Einar had been working contributed something. I cannot remember one thing about those awful days except that I was in agony, that I felt such misery I wanted to howl all the time, and even when I was silent, I was howling inside. I don't remember anything except my suffering. Even Dr. Gupta Lal can't help me remember, and besides, I don't want to. *Ahi Dio!* I was literally out of my mind. Some weeks went by. I have no idea how long I stayed at Rock Cottage, in a state of desperation, or if I ate or slept. All I can vaguely dredge up from the past is the remembrance that I did not want to stay there. I must have been given a ticket by kind Mr. Hand, or by somebody, for the next I remember, I was on the train, the Peninsula train that goes from Monterey to San Francisco.

I sat on the red plush seat and I was quiet, in dumb misery. I did not look up or out of the window. I did not see anybody, though people went by, the train stopped, people got off and others got on. I sat on, unthinking. But —I don't know at what point this happened—I became aware that someone had come and sat down next to me. It was a woman, and though I paid no attention at first, I gradually turned to look at her. She wore a long dark dress, like me, her hair was tied back with a dark silk scarf, like mine. And, though it did not startle me, or seem odd, she looked like me. But her face was kind and tranquil.

She turned and looked into my eyes and said, "La Nonna sent me. You must listen to me."

It did not seem strange that La Nonna had sent her. I was living in a dim world beyond reason then.

"Who are you?" I managed to ask, and she answered, "Margherita da Cortona."

180

I did not ponder on the fact that Margherita da Cortona had lived centuries ago. How could I? She was there, beside me, breathing, smiling.

I sat, feeling a faint stirring of ease, like the beginning of a soft dream, after hours of pain.

"You have forgotten what she told you, La Nonna," said Margherita to me. "You forgot to make penance. That is why you have lost everything you loved."

"My Nonna. I killed her," I whispered. "I broke her heart."

"She is safe now. At peace. But she grieves for you. You must make penance."

"How?" I whispered. "I have prayed and called to God, but he doesn't hear me."

"Do as I did," she answered. "Go out and work among the sick and desolate, give them a little comfort, offer them love."

She put out her hand and touched mine, and suddenly our two hands were one, and as I turned to her, she seemed to vibrate into shadow, but she came into me, and I was Margherita. I knew that she had taken up her being within mine, but I heard her voice again.

"I will be part of you; I will help you. I will guide you," she said. "And you will continue the work of penitence. Penitence."

I sat on, and a feeling of strength began to creep through me. The old prayers came to my lips with ease, and the wounds in my heart seemed to stop throbbing with pain. When the train stopped in San Francisco, I knew what I must do and where I must go.

How easy it was to find work to do! There were so many old and sick and helpless people. I found one, at once; an old woman, stumbling along the sidewalk, slipping, for the soles of her shabby furry bedroom slippers were slick and it had begun to rain. She had her head wrapped up in an old woolen scarf, her threadbare coat was held together with a big safety pin.

I went up to her and put my arm around her, to help her. She pulled away in suspicion and looked at me with terror. It was an old face, and such a sad one, because there was only fear and distrust in it.

"Let me help you," I said. "I have come to help you."

"If you could get up the stairs to my room . . ." she began, uncertain about me.

"Tell me where, and I will go with you," I told her.

"Just up this street a way. Watch out for the boy with the dog. He likes to set the dog on me, and get my meat." The old woman clutched her little parcel closer.

I saw no dog and no boy. We made our way, slowly, to where there was a narrow stairway rising upward, behind a small door with a dirty glass plane in the upper half.

Reaching into her bosom, the old woman got out a key and, looking around fearfully, to be sure nobody was coming, she opened the door and went in. I followed after. The room was small and dark, and it smelled of dirt, old cooking grease, and old humanity.

"There's a candle," the old woman mumbled. "Can't afford electricity. Or the bulbs. What for, anyhow? When it's dark, I go to bed."

I saw the bed, over against the wall. A cot, but loaded with torn, smelly bedding.

"Now, sit down and rest," I told her. I found the candle and lighted it. The old woman collapsed on the cot and stared at me, pitifully uncertain whether to fear me or trust me.

There was a tiny kerosense stove, with a little fuel still

in it; on shelves, above, were a cooking pot, a frying pan, some potatoes, and a few slices of bread.

"The water is outside, down the hall," she told me suddenly. I went to get the pot filled, and brought it back, lit the burner, and set the water on to heat.

"Do you have any tea or coffee?"

"Tea. And some meat. And a bun somebody gave me."

I took the package. The meat was coarse, with a thick rim of fat. I tried this out slowly, nudging the cooking pot over so that both could share the small flame. When the water boiled, I made her a cup of tea, and then dropped three potatoes into the hot water. She watched me patiently, and when at last, on a plate, with a fork I found, I served her a little fried meat and some boiled potatoes, she ate gratefully, mopping her old slices of bread in the grease that remained in the pan. It was all I could do with what was at hand. But she must have been half starved, to enjoy it so.

As she ate, I went to get more water, and when it was hot, I cleaned up as best I could. Then I said, "Now I'll give you a quick wash with this nice warm water and bundle you into bed, shall I?"

She was as obedient as a child. Before I had finished washing her old face and her very dirty hands, her eyelids were drooping, and soon her head flopping forward. I eased her into her bed, and she slept at once.

I stole away, blowing out the candle as I went.

I noted the number over the door, and the street.

I would need soap, a bucket, mopping cloths. More candles. Kerosene for her stove. A few essentials. Some oatmeal, I thought, and sugar. I had left her the sticky bun for her breakfast. Where would I get the money for the things I needed? Oh, it came to me at once, I would beg.

And so I did. I merely stood on a corner and held out my hand to passers-by. Most of them brushed by me. It was raining heavily, and nobody wanted to waste time. But one gave a nickel, one a quarter. In an hour's time, I had enough. A store was open, and there I bought the oatmeal and sugar, candles, and soap. I went back up then, to where my old woman slept. I entered quietly, so as not to disturb her, and I lay down on the floor. At first it was cold. But gradually I began to get warm, for after all, I was inside, out of the rain, which drummed against the dirty window. I was safe, and I had begun my penance. I offered it all to God, I crossed myself, I said my prayers, and before my eyelids, in the moments before sleep overcame me, I saw them, my darlings, my lost ones . . . Marco and Gianni . . . or Einar and Johnny Ho. No. No. Marco and Gianni. Those visions hurt too. Penance, penitence. I said my prayers again. The hurt was part of my penitence. I must accept it, hold it close, bury those awful memories under my penances. I must, and I would.

I know now that I was not always Margaret of Cortona in those first days of my penance. I reverted to plain Margaret Bardini, and then I suffered as if I were being flayed. I could not bear it, because, just as my headlong selfish love had killed La Nonna, so it had killed my Einar and my baby. If I had not been so openly eager for his love, he might have gone away, made another life. And, at Rock Cottage, night after night when I lay in his arms, I had promised and pleaded, and striven to make sure that I could keep him for myself; I had used my little Johnny Ho to hold him fast. Who was I, a young and ignorant girl, to tie him to me, a musician and creator of

184

Einar's stature? I had done it, and because I had been utterly unrepentant in my love, I had lost them. Now my penances were for them, for those three I had loved so much, and sent to their deaths, away from me.

So I thought, so I told myself, as I went about scrubbing the floor of old Mrs. Tyson's room (her name was Ella Tyson), washing her bedding, cooking a meal for her. And I did the same for other old people I found, washed up from a hard turbulent life onto a lonely shore, old people scarcely able to look after themselves, striving to survive somehow.

While I worked, offering my sore knees and tired back, my rough red hands in penance, I felt able to go on. And so I simply became Margaret of Cortona, and her life unrolled itself before me like a film. I saw her brutal father, her radiant lover. I was Margaret. I had lost my darlings, and I undertook my penitence, as the saint had done.

I could list for you all the people I tried to help, Dr. Gupta Lal. But what good would that do? I was using their poor lives to prop up my own. I know that now. I did good, I was able to apportion out some comfort, and even love, for I came to love the people I was able to help. But my penitences were essentially selfish too, weren't they? And then I began to love again . . . For instance, Ella Tyson, who somehow procured some yarn, and with her old arthritic hands crocheted a scarf for me.

And there was Marty Feld, the paralyzed child, who had to stay home, sitting in his chair, locked into the room while his mother went out to work. When I found out about them, I asked if I might have the key to open the door and be able to wash Marty and cook him something to eat. I was not given it at once; I was looked upon as an intruder. There was nothing to steal in that spare cold room, where the child sat, bundled in warm scraps of clothing. Except Marty himself. But his mother loved him, and she hated to leave him, and there was no other way to manage. She was doing the best she could.

Finally she allowed herself to trust me, and gradually she began to rely on me. And like his mother, I began to love patient little Marty, with his sudden smile, his bursts of confidence.

And then there was old Mr. Bobington, the Negro fry cook, who had only one leg, and who worked all day standing on it, until one time he fell from sheer weariness and burned himself badly.

And the stumbling hopeless derelicts who turned up in Mr. Wade's soup kitchen for something hot and the chance to lie down in a warm place.

Oh, there were so many. And I began to love them all.

This was my life for some time, three or four years. I never saw clocks, or knew what day it was. Besides, more and more completely I was living in Margaret of Cortona's flesh, and in her time. I became Margaret of Cortona in all but her sanctity. I held myself to be bad, an evil woman and an evil omen. Everything that I looked upon and loved I destroyed.

Teacher Gupta Lal, you have told me that I was Margaret of Cortona, in very truth. But how could that be, when I have lately tried so hard to be the humble girl I was born, plain Margaret Bardini? But it has seemed to me that lately, I have struggled, a war within. Part of me wants to continue as the body—the loaned body—of a saint, doing the penances she looks for, offering toil and care, and all suffering to God.

One day, when I had taken a retarded girl to Dr. Cum-

mins for an injection, I met another doctor. Dr. Francis
Sullivan. He is sensitive to suffering; he saw through my
assumed role of Helper and Comforter, to my pain and
loneliness. He began to look for me, and to accompany
me sometimes. I felt his deep sympathy, and I knew he
wanted to help me. He wouldn't give up, though I never
spoke to him.

Did he love me, perhaps? I wondered.

I began to trust him, to turn to him.

So part of me resists, and is ready, or almost ready, to
return to the real world. What causes me to rush back
into Margaret of Cortona's life is always the memory of
my sorrows and loss, and of my own guilt.

Struggling through my mind also is the startled recognition of the fact that, in the midst of my penances, undertaken to heal my conscience and my spirit, I have
begun to love, again in the old human way. I love a man,
listen for his step, long to touch him. Oh, it is love again,
like the love I knew. This seems to me to be monstrous,
unfeeling. Explain this to me, please, Teacher.

Here the transcripts ceased.

13

Dr. Sullivan read them several times, very slowly. Then
he made another appointment with Dr. Gupta Lal.

The Hindu was somewhat cool in his reception of the
doctor, and it seemed to Dr. Sullivan that he was reluctant to speak openly.

"I have come about Margaret again," said Dr. Sullivan.
"I read the transcripts and . . ."

"And you disagree with me that Margaret Bardini was used by the spirit of the saint for an interrupted, a temporary, reincarnation. I read minds. I know what you are thinking," said Dr. Gupta Lal.

"I was thinking that. But that is not important, I mean, we disagree perhaps on what Margaret experienced, but we are both happy that she has become, that she is, herself again. Are we not?"

"It is Fate. The saint could no longer use her, after I had explained that the return of Margaret of Cortona had accomplished what the lonely spirit of the saint had longed for. I am not for or against, happy or not, Fate's decrees and developments. I perceive them, I accept them. Life flows onward at all times, never static."

"Margaret calls you 'Teacher.' I can learn from you too, Dr. Gupta Lal. Please help me."

The Hindu seemed suddenly to change his attitude. Once again he became effusive, friendly, kind.

"Come with me, we will sit in the garden—I have a small garden in back here—and we will speak together," he said. His white robe flowing out around him as he hurried forward, Dr. Gupta Lal led the way. A pale sun was shining, for it had rained in the morning, and large clouds still passed fitfully across the deep blue sky. There were simple garden seats to one side. The two men sat. Dr. Gupta Lal at once seemed to fall into quietness. He sat with closed eyes, a half-smile on his lips. Dr. Sullivan was careful not to press him, or to break the gentle silence.

At last Gupta Lal spoke.

"Karma is the very energy wheel of life," he said. "It is not always understood. Karma means 'action.' If there is action, there has been cause, and there will follow an effect. This is the law of energy which rules the universe.

Wrong action brings, always, its aftermath of results, all bad also. Likewise, good action. What is good? Good is that which tends to take us one trembling step nearer the fountain of all goodness, toward Nirvana . . . selflessness, one in being with the Lord. Everything in the material world is subject to the law of karma, which is the causality that binds the physical world together. To achieve the freedom which may come after death, after many deaths, each soul must somehow convert bad karma into good, by prayers and actions.

"To do this, there are many procedures. You in the West have always tried to achieve this through penance, acts of penitence. It is certainly one way, for the holy scriptures, all of them, say we may stop the chain of karma only by sacrifice, that is, by making something holy. Or, to be more direct and simple, by acts of love."

At this point Dr. Gupta Lal fell silent and seemed to meditate for a long while. Dr. Sullivan mused on the words he had said, and waited. At last the Hindu spoke again.

"I feel that you comprehend," said Dr. Gupta Lal, looking at Francis keenly.

"I am trying to follow," answered Dr. Sullivan humbly.

"Now you want me to explain Margaret."

"Please."

"She lived out the actions of that other Margaret, who had stopped the wheel of karma with her penances," said the Hindu firmly. "This girl, so sensitive, so loving, was the appropriate shell for that other Margaret's soul to slip into. Because the saint believed that she had not made enough penances."

"But after so many centuries . . ." murmured Francis.

"There is no such thing as temporal time," said Dr. Gupta Lal firmly, "for the soul."

"So she, according to your belief, so the saint used Margaret Bardini?"

"For a time." The Hindu turned to him and smiled. "But my teaching has cleansed Margaret Bardini. The other one, who lives for penances and believes in them, may continue, somehow. Perhaps her karma is not yet complete, despite her sanctity."

"And what was the teaching that freed my . . . that freed Margaret?"

"The teaching is that one does not do penance for love. Love cancels out all penitence, for love is the approach to freedom of the soul, to eventual release into space . . . to Nirvana."

"Dr. Gupta Lal, you simplify things very easily, and you have put your finger on what all psychiatrists try to teach. There should be no guilt, there should be only a striving for understanding, and for love."

"A criminal action, of course," said the Hindu, putting the tips of his brown fingers together, "is wrong and the criminal must be separated from the world, by some means. He has entangled himself in evil karma. There was a cause for it, and there will be effects from it. The universe is netted with causality and result. This is karma. Only to a small degree are we free of karma coming down from previous lives; but to a large degree we can overbalance bad actions with good ones. And love is the lesson that, once learned, overtakes all causality, neutralizes all evil."

"I am in accord," said Dr. Sullivan. "You state what I believe. But then, you must think Margaret Bardini has learned the deepest secrets of love."

"She evidently brought them with her, from past exist-ences. Few people ever love, without counting the cost, in a manner of speaking. This is the only true love, the one which is a rehearsal for divine love, which is free, all-embracing, eternal, the love we hope to be united with, when our souls are free. Yes, that young woman was ca-pable of unselfish love, from the beginning of her life. No doubt that is why the still-unsatisfied spirit of Margaret of Cortona sought her, and lived in her for a time."

"And where is Margaret . . . Margaret Bardini now?" asked Dr. Sullivan.

"She lives near here. But she is working. If you like, I will arrange a meeting."

"I would be grateful."

14

Dr. Sullivan went to the meeting with Margaret, ar-ranged for the following week, on Sunday afternoon, as nervous as a bridegroom. How would she look, his Mar-garet, with her medieval beauty that had caught at his heart from the first? How would she behave to him? He remembered that she had left him in anger. Perhaps not anger, but rejection, surely.

He entered Dr. Gupta Lal's garden apprehensively, limping a bit more than usual, for he had returned to the hospital and had put in a heavy week of duty, and had not slept well. He was tired.

She was sitting in one of the garden chairs, wearing a dark blue dress. The sunlight was on her hair, finding coppery lights in the dark brown. She rose and came to him at once, a smile of welcome on her face.

"Dr. Frank . . . ?"

"Margaret!"

How it happened he did not know, but she had walked straight into his arms, and he held her close.

"I looked for you everywhere."

"I wanted you to find me."

"Why did you go away?"

"Because I love you, and I wanted you to love me. I couldn't bear to be just a case, anymore. And I had been fighting away that possession . . . that possession by Margherita da Cortona. She drew me back so strongly, she said words that La Nonna would have said to me. I . . . I became her, for a while. Or do you think it was all a hallucination?"

"No. I think it was a possession. A sort of angelic possession, that didn't harm you. It helped you to get through a terrible time of loss and loneliness. Whether the penances were the real reason for her possession of you, I don't know. I go only so far, with good Dr. Gupta Lal. I can accept much of his teaching. But, maybe Margaret of Cortona came into your spirit because she loved you, as I do, Margaret. Or Rita. What do you want me to call you?"

"I'm a new person. I have a new life. The girls where I work call me Peggy."

He had led her to a chair, and they sat, but he kept close hold of her hand. He lifted the hand and looked at it. He kissed the fingers.

"Is it music? The cello? Playing in an orchestra again?"

"No. I am a nurse's helper. At the hospital. I was thinking of studying nursing. I would like to work with children."

"Before we make any plans," he said quietly, lifting her

hand, and helping her rise from her chair, "there is someone we must see and speak with."

"Your mother? Oh yes. And I would like to see Gemma,
my beautiful dog. And your home."

"Your home, too. Come, let us go."

Dr. Gupta Lal appeared suddenly in the garden. He
was smiling broadly.

"No longer star-crossed lovers, I observe," he pronounced, waving his hands happily. "You see, I know
some Shakespeare also."

"Thank you, Dr. Gupta Lal, for all you have done for
me," said Peggy.

"For us both," put in Dr. Sullivan.

Holding Margaret's arm close against his side, limping
still slightly, but walking with a swift step, he led her out
through the garden and teaching rooms to where his car
waited.

15

Mrs. Sullivan heard her son's key in the lock, and she
ran from the kitchen, drying her hands on her apron. She
stopped short at sight of the couple, standing silhouetted
against the light in the hall. Margaret, and her son
Francis, her serious, solemn, reliable, quiet son. But now
his face shone with such joy that it was radiant.

"Mother, here's Margaret. I have brought her home."

"Welcome, my dear."

She kissed Margaret's smooth cheek.

"I am new, Mrs. Sullivan. A new person. Call me Peggy
now."

"Welcome, Peggy."

The three ate a simple meal together, and then Mary Sullivan retired to her bedroom with a book, and her prayers.

Peggy sat on the davenport, and when Frank came to sit beside her, favoring his leg somewhat, she turned at once into his arms again, and lifted her lips.

He kissed, once, then again.

"It is good to have you here again, home," he whispered.

"I am glad, so very glad, to be here. With you I am me. And I am safe."

"Safe, and loved."

She was silent a little space and then she said haltingly, "But when I asked you . . . when I wanted to know . . ."

"I loved you then, but I couldn't tell you."

"Oh, why? I suffered so. I had to strive to keep from falling back into that other life."

"Because I did not want the love of a sick girl, a divided heart. I wanted the whole woman. You, as you are now, and as I knew you could be."

"So you believe I am truly well, that I will not slip back once more?"

"No, you won't. Not with me at your side."

"Frank."

"Yes."

"Am I . . . unreliable, flighty . . . to love again . . . so soon? For I do love. I feel as if my whole life must be love, and with you."

"Didn't Dr. Gupta Lal teach you something about that?"

"Yes. He said love never dies. It is a continuing fountain inside one's being. When Fate removes the loved person, or object, love finds new ones. It cannot pass away or be dormant. Not true love. And he said I was one of the fortunate people who could love. *Ahi!* But love has hurt me! How I cried! How I howled! Like an animal."

"But you must not stop loving, Peggy. Love me, now."

"I do. Oh, I do! And I will. Always."

16
DR. PHILLIPS to DR. MARIAN CHESTER

". . . and it was good to hear from you, Marian. Yes, I think the study of hormonal balance, in these cases, might yield good results. We are beginning it here. It is certainly obvious that glandular imbalance affects the emotions and the mind.

"But enough of our work! We know the struggle will be endless, and maybe we will never be able to count on real cures. Let's face facts; we are a flawed species, and as medicine keeps more and more of us alive, we propagate and perpetuate our flaws.

"Gossip? Not much around here. Dr. Sullivan has finally married his Italian madonna. Greenberg gave his blessing. The girl seems well enough now. Sullivan is over the moon. I never saw anyone so happy.

"And what about you? Did I detect a note of special admiration for your new chief? I think we medical people had better marry within our own circles. Who else could stand us? So, if things come to a boil, send for me, and I'd love to be best man, or give you away, or just provide the champagne . . ."

17

They were married quietly on the lawn at Dr. Greenberg's home, under the trees, by a judge, and their plan
was to leave at once for Monterey, where they would
marry again, in the Catholic church Margaret had attended as a girl. Her father and stepmother, returned
from Italy, awaited them.

After the wedding breakfast, the embraces, and con-
gratulations, when Peggy went to change her dress, Mrs.
Greenberg came into the bedroom.

"Dr. Greenberg has a special wedding gift for you," she
said.

"Oh, but the silver bowl . . . and the coffee set that the
other doctors gave us . . . could there be something
else?"

"There is something else. Here it is."

Mrs. Greenberg put an envelope into Peggy's hands,
and then sat, on the edge of the bed, while she read it.

Peggy went to Mrs. Greenberg and kissed her.

"It is the most wonderful gift of all," she whispered. "I
will tell Dr. Greenberg so. And thank you both, for everything."

As the married couple departed in Dr. Sullivan's car,
and the guests began to disperse, Dr. Greenberg and his
wife stood on the porch together, saying goodbyes. When
the last guest had left, Mrs. Greenberg said, "It was a
pretty wedding. Do you think it will work, Joel? That girl
was once . . ."

"Was once, and may be still," said her husband. "Yes.
But I think it will work. As well as marriages ever do. It

isn't easy for two people who have been strangers to each other for more than twenty years, to take up a mutual life, in perfect accord."

"Not easy. But it can be done," said his wife, with a fond look, and she turned and kissed his cheek.